"Nick Kolakowski spins a ripping pulp yarn of smart-ass bounty hunters and bad-ass crime queenpins caught in the Jean-Claude Van God-Damnedest take on *The Most Dangerous Game* since *Hard Target*, but with no bad accents."
—Thomas Pluck, Anthony Award-nominated author of *Bad Boy Boogie*

"Bounty hunters, a Monkey Man and Zombie Bill, explosions, sharp violence and even laughs. Kolakowski brings the goods with this one!"
—Dave White, Shamus Award-nominated author of the Jackson Donne series

"A bounty hunter, his underworld criminal sister, and a dead body stuffed in a gun safe. What could possibly go wrong? Nick Kolakowski unleashes a sordid and delightfully twisted tale of double crosses, revenge, and good ol' redneck justice."
—Joe Clifford, author of the Jay Porter thrillers and *The One That Got Away*

Praise for the Love & Bullets Hookup Series

"Kolakowski's got a gift of scratching his readers' itch for pulpy, gut-wrenching narrative that moves a mile a minute and never lets you go."
—Angel Luis Colón, author of *No Happy Endings*

"Dark, bleak and in-your-face, take-no-prisoners prose, everything you want in crime fiction."
—Frank Bill, author of *Donnybrook*

BOISE LONGPIG HUNTING CLUB

NICK KOLAKOWSKI

BOISE LONGPIG HUNTING CLUB

DOWN & OUT
BOOKS

Down & Out Books
3959 Van Dyke Rd, Ste. 265
Lutz, FL 33558
www.DownAndOutBooks.com

Edited by Chris Rhatigan
Cover design by JT Lindroos

ISBN: 1-948235-13-7
ISBN-13: 978-1-948235-13-6

To R. Louie.

PART 1

A NICE PAIR OF GUNS

I

We came home from the movies to find our front door kicked open, both floors ransacked, half the food in the fridge missing. My five-year-old daughter ran into her bedroom, screaming, to make sure her toys were safe. Kelly loved her two pink princess dolls, which I won for her at the trick-shooting booth at the state fair. Her toys were safe, but when I went into my bedroom, I found that the frisky varmint had stolen my favorite things: a pair of AR-15s with expensive scopes.

First order of business: I called the cops. While I waited for them to arrive, I phoned my former brother-in-law. His voice came over the line raspy and slow, and I had to talk loudly to prevent him from nodding off. I had no compunctions about treating him a little rough, not when I paid his sister Janine a grand every month in child support, a big chunk of which probably ended up in his veins.

"Rick," I said. "You tell any of your fellow scumbags about my guns lately?"

"Nuh-uh, I swear."

If he kept to his old habits, he was in his crack shack in Garden City, near the river. "I don't believe you," I said. "Activate that chunk of meat you call a brain and think again."

I took his silence to mean he was trying his hardest. Rick had an outstanding warrant, and he knew I would roust him for it, no matter how much my ex-wife screamed at me. "Zombie Bill," he finally said.

My skin tingled. "Zombie Bill what?"

I could practically hear Rick shrug. "I told him you had a couple nice rifles. I'm sorry?"

I hung up without bothering to reply. A couple of meth freaks stealing my guns was one thing. Ten out of ten times, they would try and pawn the hardware, and end up busted. But Zombie Bill, the crazy bastard, would use those AR-15s to fill as many people with lead as possible. And that blood would be on my hands.

A police cruiser pulled into my driveway, and I walked outside to meet it, Kelly crying in my arms. The cops were polite as they took the report, and promised to do their best, which meant exactly squat.

II

Roger, my neighbor, was another firearms enthusiast. "They broke into your gun locker?" he asked, as I handed him a nylon bag loaded with enough toys, books, and snacks to see my kid through the night and the next morning.

I shook my head. "I was an idiot," I said. "I keep them in a wooden cabinet, locked."

He offered me dead eyes. "Got to get something tougher, man. Steel. Like a big safe."

"I know." I shrugged, which felt dismissive and weak. "Kept them unloaded, under lock and key. Figured that'd be enough." A gun safe with enough room for my arsenal might cost more than a thousand dollars if I wanted a good-looking one—well outside my monthly budget after I paid for the mortgage, food, gas, and the kid.

"You going to find them?"

I nodded. "It's my responsibility to make this right."

After handing Kelly over, I headed downtown in my truck. I needed to talk to Rick, and whether that discussion came with a generous beating was up to him. Zombie Bill might have stripped my house of guns, but I still had a dinky 9mm hidden inside the paperback Bible I kept in my glove compartment. Call me damned to Hell for cutting a hollow in the Good Book, and I'll tell you I'd rather risk divine wrath than show up anywhere unarmed. Besides, I lost my faith a long time ago, in a desert on the other side of the world.

Stopping at a red light, I dialed the office. Janine picked up on the first ring, sounding bored as usual. "The Bond King."

"It's your favorite bounty hunter," I said. "You want to carve time out your busy schedule, dig up a last known address?"

"You looking for a William Price?" Zombie Bill's legal name.

"What are you, psychic?"

"Nah, he called five minutes ago, said meet him at the Tastee Diner at eleven. Said you could split a basket of finger steaks or something."

"Funny guy."

"He's turning himself in?"

"Nope, he's trading info. Thanks for letting me know." I swung the truck around and headed east down West Franklin Road. The Tastee Diner, a bright and shiny temple to deep-fried fat, always had a crowd. Unless Zombie Bill planned on splattering me in front of thirty witnesses, I was probably safe there.

At the restaurant, I found a booth in the corner and took a seat facing the front door, 9mm in my left hand beneath the table. When the waitress came by, I ordered a coffee. Finger steaks are tasty, but my doctor hounded me about my cholesterol levels. At five minutes past eleven, the door opened and Zombie Bill shuffled in, dressed for success in a white T-shirt and a pair of stained cargo shorts, his tattoos resembling old wounds in the fluorescent lighting. One of his lieutenants, an inked-up skeleton with a waist-length red beard, came in behind him, taking a seat at the counter that ran the length of the restaurant.

Zombie Bill sat down across from me and smirked, revealing metal teeth that could have used a polish. "How's your night going?"

"Cut the crap," I said. "What do you want?"

He leaned back, snorted, scratched at the pink scar on his neck. He'd earned his street name after surviving eight bullet wounds to the jaw, stomach, throat, chest, and right arm. *It's like he's undead*, some halfwit had said after that. *The only way to kill him is with a shot to the brain.* "I want a favor," he said.

"Good for you. I want a new pickup and a supermodel in my bed. That doesn't mean it's going to happen. What makes you think I won't call the cops?"

"Because the cops won't ever find the guns." Zombie Bill waggled a bony finger at me. "You think I'm an idiot? Why you keeping that much firepower around the house, anyway?"

"What can I say, I believe in home defense," I said, my stomach knotting.

"I'm not asking anything of you that I wouldn't do myself," he said, flashing those teeth I so desperately wanted to yank out of his head. "Just that you don't bust me or my crew. Maybe sometimes I ask you to track someone down, and you do it."

"I'm never getting those weapons back, am I?" I said. "It's like endless collateral for you."

Bill bit his lip. "What's 'collateral' mean?"

"I'm dealing with a genius here."

He slapped the table. "This genius already got a task for you: Frankie has some outstanding warrants."

"No," I said. "You know I can't do that."

"Can't, or won't?"

"Same difference."

He slapped the table again, harder. "Better think that over," he said. "When you're ready to make a deal, you call that number I left at your office. I'm giving you until tomorrow afternoon, maybe. Then I do something real bad." And he left, the red lieutenant drifting in his wake, while around me a lot of nice people went on clogging their veins with delicious fat, oblivious to the weird horrors happening all around them.

III

Frankie stood five-foot-two in her customary combat boots, her small body tight with muscle and sharp with bone. She wore as much black clothing and eyeliner as a high school Goth, and nobody made jokes about it, because she liked to do things like shove pens through necks. As she poured me a whiskey, she said, "My old friend Bill."

"Wants you arrested," I said.

"Yeah, so one of his little meth-head bitches can shank me inside. He can't beat me on the street, you know."

"I didn't say he wasn't predictable." I sipped the whiskey, checking out her new office: a shipping container with a skylight cut in the roof, a thick rug on the floor, a leather couch at one end, and a nice desk at the other. The container sat at the edge of the river. Anyone who wanted to take a shot at her would have to bypass three fences and ten bodyguards. Frankie had founded an e-commerce site on the darknet that exchanged Bitcoin for pretty much anything illegal, which meant hundreds of powerful people in twenty countries wanted her cold on a slab, all for different reasons. Hence the security, and her habit of wearing a bullet-resistant vest around Boise, one of the safest cities in America.

"Bill's not predictable, is the problem. Never stops moving." She slugged down her drink. "Thanks for calling me about it."

"You know I didn't have a choice," I said.

"True." She poured herself another round, after topping off my half-full glass. "Now drink up, because you're not going to like the solution I'm offering. You'll have to abuse the powers of your office."

IV

I've done a lot of bad things in my life, but I've never felt scummier than the next morning when I paid bail for Mark Miller, accused of carnal relations with a variety of barn animals. He was the sort of simpering scumbag who makes you fear for the future of the human race. As we exited the jail, he kept asking me who I was and what I wanted. I don't think of myself as blood simple, but it felt like sweet relief once we made it to my truck, where I could punch him in the face many, many times until he snapped into unconsciousness.

You want to know the worst part? I had paid a lot of cash to spring him loose, and I would probably never see a dime of it again.

It was noon by the time I finished cleaning my knuckles, and with Miller bound and gagged in my back seat I swung by the office. Janine, who never seemed to leave her desk, gave me Zombie Bill's number. I dialed it in the parking lot, the only place where I had a modicum of privacy.

"You arrest Frankie?" he asked.

"Nope," I said, injecting my voice with false cheer. "But guess who I just sprung from jail?"

He knew. Even with someone like Zombie Bill, there are only so many cousins you can have locked up at one time, especially if the cousins in question help you run your drug-smuggling business. It took him forever to speak. "You making a play here?"

"Uh, yeah. Duh. You hand over my guns, you get your relative back. If you act fast, I might leave most of his face intact. If you don't, he's going to tell me enough to make your life real difficult, and real short."

"I will kill your daughter," he said. "I will blow her brains the fuck out."

My vision went red, and it took superhuman control to force the next words through my clenched jaw without screaming. "She's already out of the city. You want to blast my ex-wife, though, you go right ahead and save me another thirteen years of child support." That part about the kid was true: my friendly neighbor Roger and his girl-friend had driven my little pumpkin north to their cabin.

Zombie Bill fell silent again, so I took the initiative. "Listen, man, your plan wasn't a bad one, but it's over. Give me the rifles, and I'll hesitate to bust you in the future. Scout's honor. Otherwise, this all just ends in blood."

Something in my voice convinced him. "You know the big quarry in the foothills, the kids call it the Hole? Meet me there in two hours. Bring my idiot cousin."

"Bring my guns."

V

When we were teenagers, we used to bike up to the Hole on hot summer days, and dare each other to jump into its watery depths, to risk our spines in the name of applause and a couple dollars. A few plunged into the depths of the quarry and never surfaced. Later on, it served as a favorite dumping ground for snitches, and a few of my clients ended up there.

I had Mark Miller on his knees near the edge of the chasm, blindfolded, with my 9mm pressed against the back of his neck. I watched as Zombie Bill's monster truck maneuvered through the open gate in the chain-link fence surrounding the quarry, wondering whether I'd made a huge mistake, if my old self—the one who'd survived countless shootouts and standoffs in Baghdad—had whispered too much bad advice from deep in my subconscious.

The truck stopped maybe fifty yards away, skewed so it pointed back toward the gate. Zombie Bill and his lieutenant climbed out, Zombie Bill's hands empty of rifles.

I cocked back the hammer on the 9mm. "I'm not messing with you," I said.

"Where's your backup?" Zombie Bill asked, scanning the empty quarry. "You didn't come alone, did you?"

I dug the pistol into Miller's head. "I'll start counting to three."

Zombie Bill raised his hands, palms out. "Relax, your stuff's in the back seat there. I just got to check. You okay, cuz?"

Another man climbed out of the far side of the truck: bearded, black sunglasses, forearms needled with flaming skulls. He walked to the right, worrying my flank.

"I'm good," Miller said. "Just get me the hell out of here."

"Why don't you walk him over?" Zombie Bill called out. "We had a deal, right?"

"Why don't you call your dog over here off?" I said, turning my head to keep an eye on roving Mister Skull.

Zombie Bill said nothing. Mister Skull kept moving. I had boxed myself in. Sure, I could have leapt into the abyss to my left, and risked my spine, if the mining company hadn't drained the water from it years ago.

So much for keeping things nice and civil, I thought, swiveling my gaze to the cliff that walled one side of the quarry.

The back of Mister Skull's head exploded, followed a quarter-second later by the sound of a gunshot echoing off stone.

Miller, blind and panicked, did a stupid thing: rocketing to his feet with surprising quickness, he tried kicking me in the groin. I sidestepped easily, losing my grip on him—and he decided to run away.

Pro tip: When sprinting a one-hundred-meter dash in a quarry, make sure to remove any blindfold first. He plunged over the edge of the hole, his legs bicycling in space, and Zombie Bill's scream of rage couldn't quite drown out the crunch of one hundred fifty pounds of pervert hitting granite at terminal velocity.

I raised the 9mm and emptied the magazine in Zombie

Bill's direction, then ran for an inviting patch of rocks a few yards away. A black SUV bounced down a dirt ramp that led from the cliffs, screeching to a halt beside me. The front passenger door popped open, revealing Frankie in a camouflage outfit, rifle in her arms.

"We got to stop them," I yelled at her. "They get out of here, I'm screwed." Zombie Bill and his lieutenant had made it inside the truck, which lurched into gear—bullets sparking off its bumper as Frankie fired off a burst—and promptly crashed into the chain-link fence at the edge of the quarry.

Frankie's laughter came deep and ominous as a thundercloud. She raised a hand above her head and snapped her fingers twice. "Monkey Man," she called out.

The rear door of the SUV opened, and out climbed a man in an unmarked blue jumpsuit, his face covered by a cheap rubber chimpanzee mask so large, it shaded his eyes into black holes. He had a long metal tube cradled in his arms.

"You can't be serious," I said.

"That's what I love about you," Frankie said. "You're all upset about your guns and shit, meanwhile I'm buying artillery online."

As the Monkey Man approached, he grasped the ends of the metal tube and pulled, extending it. Stopping beside us, he flicked up a tiny metal sight on the tube's end, placed the hardware on his shoulder, and cocked his head toward Frankie.

"Put your fingers in your ears," she said, and I did as ordered. The Monkey Man swiveled, the tube tracking Zombie Bill's truck as it struggled to pull free of the collapsed fence, its rear wheels tangled in wire. Through the windshield, we saw Zombie Bill fumbling with one of my rifles, while his lieutenant shrieked and punched the steering wheel.

The Monkey Man pulled the trigger on the underside of the tube, and the air around us exploded. A white plume of death rocketed across the quarry and impacted the rear of the truck, lifting it into the air on a pillar of flame, the doors blasting open to eject burning Bill and the lieutenant. I felt a little sorry for the two of them. Roasted alive is a pretty horrible way to die. But then again, so is overdosing on the crappy drugs Bill sold.

The truck crumpled back to Earth in a shower of sparks, the dull thud of its impact bouncing off the quarry walls. The Monkey Man returned to the SUV, whistling a merry tune, swinging the launcher around like a prop in an old-time musical. While we waited for the flames to die down, Frankie pulled a crumpled pack of menthol cigarettes from the back pocket of her jeans, lit one, and puffed with the great satisfaction of someone doing a sinful thing. "How's my niece?" she asked.

"Good," I said. "She loved that castle toy thing you got her."

"Excellent. I hope it gives her ideas about ruling the world." She took another puff, blasted smoke out her nose. "Because our family, it's all about power, you know? Or we're crushed."

"I just find people," I said.

"You're covering my flank on the lawful side," she replied, punching me softly in the shoulder. "But you're just as much a part of this. You know, I spent a year trying to get Bill out of hiding."

"Good thing he just happened to rob me, huh?" I began

walking toward the truck, figuring the fire had quieted enough for me to see whether I could grab my guns before any law showed up. The air smelled like a gasoline-fueled barbeque.

"Yeah, I figured you wouldn't let him blackmail you." Following in my footsteps, Frankie paused long enough to crush the finished cigarette beneath her heel. "I have a confession."

"Oh, crap."

"I told Rick to tell Bill's people about the guns."

"Damn it, sis."

"He bought from Bill once a week. It was a calculated risk, okay? I told Rick when you were going to the movies."

"What'd you give Rick?" I stopped twenty feet away from the truck, glancing once at Bill, who looked like something left on the grill an hour too long. No bullet in the head required after all. The blast had tossed one of my AR-15s nearby; the other, as far as I could tell, had merged with the twisted metal that had once been the truck's cab.

"Told him I'd pay to send him to rehab. He's ready to go. And I figured that'd get you points with your ex."

"Just as long as she doesn't hear about all this." I slung my surviving rifle over my shoulder. "Give me a ride home? I got to cook dinner for my little girl."

"Bro, seriously, it's the least I can do. You just made me queen of this town."

PART 2

TOO MANY BODIES

I

I was ten miles east of home when the cover blew off the sixteen-foot tri-hull hitched to my truck. As it flapped down the highway like a bright blue ghost, the slipstream scooped my fishing tackle, empty beer cans, paper-towel rolls, and other crap from the bottom of the boat and hurled the whole caboodle at the car behind me. The car swerved into the middle lane, dodging the debris, which was the good news. It doesn't take much to smash a windshield, not to mention a driver's forehead.

The bad news: the other car was a police cruiser.

And, boy, did I piss off the cop driving it.

I pulled onto the shoulder, lowered my window, and set both hands on the sill, crossed at the wrist, driver's license and registration and concealed-carry permit in my right. He exited the cruiser roaring curses, and I worried he wouldn't hear me when I announced the .45 automatic tucked in my glove compartment.

"I'm carrying, but I got a license," I called out, offering my sunniest smile. "I'm a bounty hunter."

"That so?" The tag on his chest said his name was Varney. He had close-cropped gray hair and a face as lined as an acre of sun-scorched dirt. The short walk between the cruiser and my truck had calmed him a tad, but a vein in his reddened forehead ticked like a bomb. I get along with most cops but something about this guy made it hard to keep my lips in the upright and locked position. Maybe it was the way he kept touching his sidearm.

"Yes, sir," I said. "Sorry about the cover and my gear. I can leave my vehicle and pick it up, if that's okay with you. I think it all went into that ditch over there."

"Stay in your vehicle," he snapped. "You want to go to jail today?"

"No, sir."

"Then let me see your licenses there."

I handed over the documents. "You from Boise?" he asked.

"Yes, sir."

"You Frankie's kin?"

No sense in lying—he could ring up my family history on the laptop in his cruiser. "That's correct. I'm her baby brother."

"I thought I recognized the name. You know, we're going to nail her one day." Varney sounded almost wistful. "She must think she's the Queen Turd of this particular pile of poop, but I'm here to tell you, we've flushed a lot of her kind. And if I'm remembering right, you're not so clean yourself."

What a darling metaphor, I almost said, but that vein in his forehead kept throbbing and I had no urge to end my day in handcuffs. Instead I waited for him to either give me a ticket or cut me loose. An eighteen-wheeler roared past, its wind buffeting my boat.

The vein settled beneath the cop's skin. He spat into the gravel between his boots. "I apologize for what I just said," he said, as he stared somewhere beyond my right shoulder. "We're all on edge here. You hear about that shooting at the Quik-Stop last night, over near Parma?"

I nodded. The morning news had spent every second on it. Two clerks and a bystander shot dead by assailants unknown, who took off with the forty-three dollars in the register and a six-pack of beer. The bystander was a teenage boy named Charles Beevoir, a football star at one of the local high schools, and the news flashed his smiling mug in a corner of the screen every few minutes. No word on whether the security camera above the register had recorded anything of use.

"Shooters are a couple of cold critters, and they're still at large," Varney said, handing back my documents. "So we're keeping an eye out. You happen to hear anything in your travels, you give us a call, okay?"

"Will do," I said, wondering whether to raise the delicate matter of my boat cover and fishing tackle in the ditch. The cop's hard look suggested I should leave that topic unmentioned for the time being. "I appreciate you not ticketing me over this."

"I'd call it professional courtesy," he smirked, "but as far as I'm concerned, bounty hunters are one small step above the scum you're catching. Don't think about picking up your litter right now. It's rush hour, I don't want rubberneckers slowing the road up."

Maybe he expected me to lose my cool. Instead I offered him a wink. "You have a good day, Officer."

He strode back to his cruiser without a word. When his taillights disappeared around the next bend, I started my engine and rejoined the flow of traffic. I would wait until dark to drive back for my stuff, because instinct told me that Varney was the sort of sadist who would take the next exit and swing back around, just to catch me standing in the ditch. Besides, I had a pair of cleaned trout in a cooler in the back seat, and an overpowering urge to fire up my grill, pop a beer, and settle on my porch chair in time for sunset. I wanted done with this day.

But the day wasn't done with me. Not by a long shot.

II

It had already been a terrible week. On Monday, the merry folks at The Bond King asked me to pick up a man named Scott Parson, who in no way fit the usual profile of a bail jumper: forty-five years old, with a developer job at a local software company, no previous arrests on his record, and not a firearm to his name.

Scott Parson had a dead kid, thanks to an idiot teenager named Stephen Marshall. One April night, Marshall downed ten cans of beer, climbed behind the wheel of his millionaire father's monster truck, and hit the highway at a hundred miles an hour with his headlights off. He rear-ended Parson's minivan, crumpling both vehicles to scrap metal. Parson's six-year-old son, sleeping in the rear seat, died instantly.

Marshall's father Jim hired the best lawyers, who claimed in court that their young client suffered from "affluenza," meaning he was too much of a wealthy prick to know right from wrong. The court sentenced Marshall to ten years of probation, no jail time.

Following the verdict, with a reporter's microphone jammed in his face, Parson promised to kill the kid who murdered his son. The court charged him with criminal threat. How's that for fair, given his traumatized state of mind? And when Parson, out on bail, failed to show up for a hearing, he became my target.

Sometimes I hated my job.

People have an image of bounty hunters as Old West cowboys who kick down doors, guns ready, and pop anyone who draws down on them. As with most jobs, the reality is a lot more boring. Although I always made a point of strapping on a bullet-resistant vest while on the clock, many of my professional colleagues wore nothing more protective than a T-shirt. The vest had Bail Enforcement Agent stenciled on the front and back, which always guaranteed that, when I entered certain neighborhoods, some people on the street turned and ran at the sight of me.

Many of my colleagues also carried tasers or pepper spray instead of guns. One old friend, Rooster Marley, opted for a wooden baseball bat, which can prove a useful combination of door-basher and skull-cracker. Not me. I had a firearm on my hip, with a backup rifle in the trunk of my vehicle. Ninety-nine percent of the time, the mere presence of a weapon made bail jumpers come quietly.

One of Parson's coworkers told me that he had holed up in a residence in Caldwell, a small town down the highway from Boise. *He bought it so he could rent it out*, the guy said. *Before, you know, the thing with his kid.* The address was on a steep hill of worn-out houses with weedy yards and sagging chain-link fences.

Parson had no military experience, no criminal record before his arrest, nothing that led me to believe he would pose much of a threat when I found him. His mugshot suggested a man whose idea of exercise was lifting a can of beer to his mouth. I took my pistol anyway. Better safe than sorry.

The rear of Parson's rental property had a high wooden fence in need of repair. Standing on my toes, I peeked into a backyard bristling with cheatgrass and thorny bushes. A sun-faded kiddie pool leaned against the splintery excuse for a porch. I saw no water bowls or other signs of a dog, and that was good. Nothing can ruin a morning like a pooch deciding to take a chunk of meat out of your ass.

I circled to the front. No gate barred me from walking up to the front door. The dusty picture window to my left had its curtains drawn. I knocked. No answer.

I knocked again. Out of the corner of my eye, I saw the curtains flutter. A faint thump from the other side of the door. I knew what that sound meant.

Leaping off the stoop, I sprinted around the side of the house, my hand on my holster. I reached the back fence as Parson scrambled atop it, the wood crackling under his soft weight. He cried out as I gripped his collar and pulled as hard as I could, sending him crashing to the dirt. Before he took a fresh breath, I had him on his stomach, a pair of plastic riot-cuffs binding his wrists behind his back.

"You have to let me go," he wheezed. "I got a job to do."

In between gulps of oxygen, I said: "You're going back to jail."

"It's not fair," he said, stronger, twisting his head to stare me down.

I checked his restraints as an excuse to look away from that burning gaze. "It's just my job, man."

"You got kids?"

I hoisted him upright, my muscles screaming for mercy. Parson could afford to lose a few pounds. "That's not your problem," I said.

"What would you do in my position?" A tear trickled

down his cheek. "What would you do?"

I placed a hand in the middle of his back and guided him toward my truck at the end of the block. His head slumped, and his shoulders sagged. Opening the passenger door, I eased him into the seat. Sometimes you need to really secure a prisoner before escorting them to jail, but Parson seemed cored out.

"I failed as a father," he said, spittle flecking his lips.

"That's not true," I said, starting the truck. "The fact that he passed away—and I'm sorry about that—got nothing to do with you. I'm sure you did a fine job."

"You got kids?"

"Doesn't matter." I pulled away from the curb, anxious to deposit this man in jail and head home. I wanted to wrap Kelly in my arms, feel her warm and alive and breathing. I dreaded what this man might say next to spark my fears.

Parson rested his cheek against the window, staring with eyes like burned-out lightbulbs at his rental house sliding past. "I spent so much time here, trying to fix that place up," he said. "Before you showed up, I was going to set it on fire."

"Why?"

He shrugged as if his shoulders were made of concrete. "Because it didn't matter," he said, and stayed quiet for the rest of the ride.

After a Monday like that, I reserved a little time later in the week for fishing.

My incident with Varney cost me a few minutes on the highway, and that, combined with a traffic jam near my exit, meant I pulled into my driveway a half-hour later than expected. I parked the truck on its concrete pad beside the garage, shut off the engine, and paused to watch the fields beyond the house shimmering golden in the setting sun. A view like that always made me happy to be alive, no matter what.

Everyone needs space from the rest of humanity, and selling our old house in Boise had provided enough for a down payment on four acres on the Idaho side of the Snake River, far from the nearest town. The land came with a two-story house and a couple of small outbuildings. I kept telling people that one day I would use the back fields for crops and cattle, but given my busy schedule, they would probably land a man on Mars before I got around to building a proper farm.

I retrieved the pistol from the glove compartment, slipped it in the holster on my belt, tucked the fish cooler under my arm, and exited the truck. Uncoupling the boat from the hitch could wait until after dinner. I trotted for the backyard and my grill with the focus of a heat-seeking missile.

Janine, my once and future wife, sat on the back porch, squeezing a plush orange stress ball so hard I saw the tendons in her forearm popping from twenty feet away.

"Long day?" I asked.

"Like you wouldn't believe," she said. "Caterer is trying to hose us."

"I thought we locked that down."

The stress ball bulged between her bloodless fingers. "Dude called back today, said they didn't know they'd have to come all the way out here. Said that's a price increase."

Janine and I planned on getting remarried in the yard behind our house. It would be an upgrade from our first go-round, at City Hall on a random Monday, a week after we discovered she was pregnant with our little bundle of joy. But as we soon discovered, planning a wedding in the middle of nowhere is a logistical nightmare on the level of D-Day.

"Tell them we'll get someone else," I said.

"There is nobody else," she said through gritted teeth. "We settled on these people. They're the only ones with decent food, remember?"

"Sorry, babe." I dropped the cooler beside our jumbo gas grill. "Maybe we just bite the bullet on it, cut costs in some other area. We'll look at the spreadsheet, okay?"

Janine growled.

"I had a hard day," I said, hoping that would shut down the conversation.

"You went *fishing.*"

"Yeah, because it was a miserable week," I said. "Then, coming back from the lake, the boat cover flies off, and I get pulled over by some cop. He gave me some real attitude, too. I like to think I get along with cops, but not in this case."

"You get the cover back?"

"No, the cop wouldn't let me pick it up. Some other stuff blew out, too. I'll drive out and get it after we eat." I twisted the grill's knobs and pushed the little red button that ignited the flames.

"We got the Johnsons tonight," she said. "We can go after that."

I frowned. "We can't dodge?"

"We dodged four times already. We're trying to be more neighborly, remember?"

"Yes. More neighborly. Got it." I opened up the porch cooler, a red monstrosity with a weather-beaten lid, and retrieved a pair of tall cans from the sea of meltwater inside.

"You don't have to talk much." Tossing the stress ball into the nearest chair, Janine flexed the looseness back into her hand. I handed her a beer, which she set on the glass table beside the cooler. "Thanks. I'll get the dinner stuff."

After she disappeared inside the house, I downed half my brew and surveyed my vast domain. I kept the yard mowed tighter than a crewcut, while letting the fields beyond the box-wire fence sprout wild. The middle of nowhere felt like a paradise after that Boise cul-de-sac where our first marriage had imploded.

Janine returned to the porch with a basket of paper plates, condiments, cups, unlit candles, and plastic table-ware. "Cut you a lemon," she said, handing the slices over.

"Thank you, ma'am. You hear from our little tyke today?"

"Yeah, she's good. Grandma has her sugared up." Kelly was staying with my mother in Montana for a few weeks.

"Good," I said. "I'll send her an email later."

"She doesn't do email anymore." Janine announced in a serious tone. "Now it's this messaging app, lets you put little colored rainbows and cartoons all over the screen."

"Great. Now I have to learn something new. I can barely type."

She smirked as she popped open her beer. "Want to hear something else that's funny?"

"Hell yes."

Taking a seat on the edge of the porch, her legs kicking in space, she said: "So I'm in the bathroom at work, and I hear someone else come in. They take the stall next to mine, but I can't see feet, so I'm not quite sure who it is. They pull down their pants, and I hear the most godawful sounds ever. Take the worst poop you can imagine and multiply it by a hundred. Like a wildebeest being slaughtered. And whoever it is, they're grunting. Loud. Over and over again. Luckily I'm finishing my own business, so I can wipe up and head out of there, pronto. Except."

I chuckled. "Except."

She shook her head. "Except my OCD starts telling me: 'You must wash each finger on your hands ten times, then touch the sink knobs twenty times each, or you can't leave.' And you know I can't ignore that little voice. I'm standing there, scrubbing my fingers raw, more and more frantic by the second, because if those sounds from the toilet stop and that person comes out, God help us both, we'll never see each other in the same way, you know? There'll be too much history."

I opened the grill lid and hovered my hand an inch above the hot metal. Nearly ready. "So what happened?"

"There's this fart from the stall, so loud I'm deafened," she said. "Then comes the flush. I'm four seconds away from this person coming out but I've done my twenty taps on the knobs and I have a paper towel in my hand and I just sprint for the door. I don't look back, I do not pass go, I just run into the hallway. Disaster averted. Because you know, with my luck, it was probably my boss."

"Oh, probably." This is marriage, I thought. Two people comfortable talking about farts and poops. If you ask an immature bastard like me, it's so much more relaxing than dating, when everybody has to pretend their shit doesn't stink.

"What's that?" Janine asked.

I turned to see her pointing at something small and shiny at the edge of the yard, beside one of the fence-posts.

Funny how I hadn't noticed it a minute ago. Dusk has a way of playing tricks with your vision.

"Hold on," I said, climbing off the porch. My hand whispered over my holster. When I reached the fence, I flicked the grass away with my heel, revealing a silver pendant necklace clotted with mud. I picked it up, winding the chain around my right thumb. The pendant was shaped like a heart, with two letters engraved on its front: RJ. I scanned the tall grass on the far side of the fence, ears straining for anything louder than the rustling grass.

"What was it?" Janine called behind me.

"Some piece of jewelry. Not yours." Our neighbor's home sat to our left, at the distant bend of the river. It was a dump, a cinderblock box with a tin roof, but the man who owned it did a good job of keeping his dogs off my property. I chose to ignore when his brother, who had several outstanding warrants for petty crimes, stopped by for a few beers every Sunday afternoon.

No dogs or trucks in front of his place. He must have been hunting.

"Whose is it?" she asked.

"I don't know," I said, a little too sharply. "I've never seen it before. Maybe a bird dropped it."

"Okay, okay." She turned away. "I want to eat, please."

We ate dinner on the porch by candlelight. As much as I tried to act relaxed, I kept eyeballing the fields, which made Janine fidget. I felt awful when she scraped aside the last of her fish and, without a word, stomped inside to wash up. The last of the sun died behind the hills, staining the sky a bruised purple that quickly darkened to black. In the murk beyond the river, a few isolated lights twinkled to life.

While Janine worked at the sink, I headed through the door at the far end of the kitchen. The room beyond was windowless, the clean fluorescent light glinting off my weight racks and freestanding chin-up bar, along with the enormous gun safe I had slotted in the far corner.

Unlike my wooden cabinet in the old house, this beautiful black box was impervious to anything short of a shaped charge. It had cost me two thousand dollars, but its deep interior could hold ten rifles. Right now, the only racked guns included my fine Beretta twelve-gauge (for skeet shooting), my Mossberg Tactical with the pistol grip (which made it an awkward weapon for home defense, no matter what anyone tells you—I had taken it in lieu of cash payment for an off-the-books skiptrace), my remaining AR-15, and three pistols in a wire rack. Locked drawers on the bottom held boxed ammunition, a few hundred dollars in crisp twenties, stacks of clay targets, my orange hunting vests, and a couple of yellowed teeth that had special significance to me. Dragging the heavy door open, I dropped the silver necklace in the top drawer before closing the safe again.

My hand against the cold metal, I shuddered.

III

After I unhitched the boat from the truck, we drove the mile down the road to the Johnson house. Janine wrapped her fingers in mine and squeezed hard. "Think we've had enough beers to face this?" she asked.

"No."

We pulled into the long driveway of a two-story McMansion with a commanding view of the river, its windows ablaze with light. These houses had sprung up across southern Idaho in recent years, bought by rich Californians and Texans in the market for a second or third home. They might have enjoyed the state's low taxes and stunning landscape, but I often wondered what they thought about living next door to folks who barely scraped by.

Having grown up in a household with no money, the sight of expensive boats and cars parked within a stone's throw of chicken coops and collapsing double-wides always filled me with rage. As I braked alongside a late model BMW parked in front of the garage, I mimed stomping on the gas, as if to plow our three tons of metal through that wedding-cake monstrosity of a house. Janine slapped my shoulder. "Behave," she said.

"It's okay," I said. "I'm not taking the firearm with me."

The front door opened, and a short man with a small gray goatee and a round gut appeared on the stoop. He wore a stained sweatshirt with Harvard across the front in big red letters, a pair of blue basketball shorts, and a scuffed pair of Crocs. "Howdy!" he called, waving a large, soft hand.

His wife appeared in the doorway: blonde, pretty in a long pink housedress and shiny high heels. She wrapped a yoga-toned arm around his waist.

"Quick, tell me again," I whispered as we waved back. "What are their names?"

"Rob and Susan."

"Just shoot me now."

Janine poked me in the ribs and climbed out. I took my sweet time pulling the key from the ignition and locking up. I had difficulty believing our neighbors had ever faced a day of trouble in their lives—real trouble, I mean, the kind that leaves you feeling as if someone scraped out your guts with a big spoon.

After shaking hands and guiding us into a kitchen roughly the size of an airplane hangar, Rob poured us towering glasses of Merlot. "We're just up here for two weeks," he said, after making a big show of swirling his wine and sniffing it. "Last-minute sort of deal. Good thing I can run the business from my phone, you know?"

I noted a pair of high-powered MacBooks on the marble kitchen counter, beside a tall stack of papers. "What do you do?"

"Big Data," he said. "I lead a team that designs algorithms that box stores use to manage inventory, figure out when to drop prices, stuff like that. It's a lot of Apache Hadoop work, because we're wrestling with petabytes of data."

36

"Huh," I said. "You up here for the Big Data?" The words sounded stupid coming out of my mouth.

"Nah, a little hunting," he said. "Friend of mine wanted to shoot some game."

"Weird time of year for it." Deer season was a couple months away.

He flicked a hand. "Oh, I don't know what he wants to hunt. I just wanted an excuse to come up, know what I mean?"

"How long have you been married?" Susan asked.

"Five years, the first time around," Janine said, hooking her arm around my elbow and rubbing my bicep. "We're prepping for a second go-round this summer, big wedding in the backyard."

"Oh, like renewal vows?" Rob chimed in. "Susan and I were thinking of that. Show our friends and family we'd do the whole crazy ride again in a heartbeat."

"No, we got divorced before," Janine said, making her voice extra-sweet and bubbly. "Totally nasty. We really tried to ruin each other. But we got over it."

Rob stared at his feet, and I sipped my wine. It tasted like spoiled grape juice. Why spend thirty bucks on a bottle of this crap when you could buy a six-pack of good beer for half that? I would never understand rich folk.

"Who wants the grand tour?" Susan said, breaking into a little dance number in her high heels as she gestured for us to follow her through the nearest doorway.

With a sullen Rob bringing up the rear, we hiked the first floor, pausing every few seconds so Susan could point out another pricey element: stainless-steel fridges with touch-screens built into the doors, Japanese knives atop the maple butcher block, giant televisions behind sliding panels, and enormous paintings on the walls that looked like clown vomit. Through the kitchen windows I sighted a standalone hot tub sunk into the wraparound porch. In one hallway, I almost tripped over an orange Dyson vacuum cleaner parked like a dead droid. And you bet I noticed the top-notch security system, just in case any neighbors decided to engage in a little wealth redistribution.

Did the sight of those expensive toys make me jealous? Absolutely. I consoled myself with the idea that I could beat Rob in a fair fight. You can't buy grit.

I kept glancing at Janine, noting the tension in her face. Houses without books always made her unsettled, and there was nary a hardcover or paperback in sight, much less a bookshelf. Lord knows, if you managed to somehow hoist our own humble abode onto a scale, half its weight would come from printed pages.

"Jake," Susan asked me, as we paused in the living room. "What is it you do for a living? I don't think Rob mentioned it."

"I'm a bounty hunter," I said, keeping my face neutral as her eyebrows shot up.

"Oh, is that dangerous?" she asked.

"Not as much as you'd think," I said. "Mostly it's just driving around, picking up deadbeats. I only have to break someone's arm once or twice a week."

The corner of Susan's mouth twitched.

"That was a joke," I said, saluting her with my wineglass.

Susan made a heroic attempt at smiling. "Do you know anything about those murders the other night? At that gas station?"

I shook my head. "I don't talk to the police that often. All I know is what I've seen on the news. There's been a lot of coverage, so I expect they'll catch the guy."

"I hope so," Susan said. "We come out here to relax, not jump at every little sound."

How difficult for you, I thought, glancing at my wife. From the set of her jaw, it was clear she had run out of patience with our new neighbors. "What do you do for money, Susan?" Janine asked.

It was Susan's turn to stare at her feet. "A little of this and that."

"How nice," Janine said, flashing her teeth.

Quick as a linebacker intercepting a football, Rob leaned into the conversation and clinked his glass against mine. "Want to follow me to the garage, buddy? Got something cool to show you."

Susan already had a hand on Janine's shoulder, guiding her toward another wing of the house. My wife, who hated strangers touching her, kept her expression neutral as they disappeared around a corner. Why had we decided on this meet-the-neighbors crap in the first place? Downing half my wine, I followed Rob down a short hallway.

"Gotta apologize for Susan," Rob said in a low tone, once we were alone.

"Huh?"

"She gets annoying." He rolled his eyes.

"She's fine." What kind of man complains about his wife to a stranger?

"She's just excited. You can actually hold a conversation. Not like those rednecks next door—you probably know them—the Masons?" Opening the door in front of us, Rob stepped aside and beckoned for me to enter.

"I know them." And I bet they hate your guts, I thought. Between the two of them, the Masons held down five jobs and a houseful of kids, goats, and dogs. They had no time for fancy wine or Big Data.

Rob followed me into the cleanest three-car garage I had ever seen: no oil stains on the smooth concrete floor, no posters or paint-blotches on the walls, no grime on the tool-boxes lined neatly on the spotless worktable. The bluish fluorescents gleamed liquidly on the flank of an orange Pontiac GTO parked in the center space.

"That's a real pretty car, Rob." I ran my palm along the hood, leaving a faint grease stain. Whoops.

If Rob saw how I defaced his chariot, he chose not to mention it. "Picked it up from this vintage-car place down in Anaheim, where we got our other home. I told my wife that I was just going to look around, that I'd be a good boy, and I walk out thirty minutes later with a contract. And I swear, I really was just going to look." He chuckled. "But then I caught sight of this baby and I just couldn't resist."

"I also got that problem."

He looked confused. "What?"

"With buying vintage automobiles."

Rob stared at me, and I wondered whether I had crossed some sort of line. Then his face split in a wide grin. "Yeah, I've been lucky in life, I can't deny it." Luckier than some people in this room, his tone said.

"What are the specs?" Everybody loves talking specs.

"It's a 1970, long-stroke four-five-five, four-speed transmission, three-point-three-one axle," he chanted, as if reading from a manual. "Zero to sixty in six seconds."

"You take it out? Do a little drag-racing?"

"Oh yeah, I go up against the kids in their Hondas all the time," he said, laughing. "No, I hardly take it out.

Trying to keep it quality, you know? Wouldn't want to ding anything. We need to run errands, we take the BMW."

"It's a beautiful car."

"Thank you. Maybe we can take a ride in it sometime." He slapped me on the shoulder. "When that happens, I'll drive."

The kinder part of me resisted the urge to smack him back. Instead I leaned through the Pontiac's open window and ran my hand over the pebbled leather wheel. The interior was a museum display of old-school dials and buttons. Gorgeous. I pictured myself in the driver's seat, crashing through that garage door and gone before Rob could so much as yell, the engine roaring loud enough to rip the sky in half, all my problems disappearing in the rearview mirror.

"Thanks for the tour," I said, standing straight. "But my wife and I got to head out."

Rob frowned. "You're serious? You just got here."

I nodded. "Sorry. Got to deal with a mess left by a cop."

IV

In another lifetime, I might have become a cop myself. People would have said I was following a family tradition.

My daddy was a deputy in the days before meth poisoned this country to its core. As a kid, I worshipped him as the second coming of Wyatt Earp. Whenever he came home after a shift I would sit on his bed and watch with religious awe as he stripped off his scuffed leather duty belt and unloaded his pistol before locking both items in his bureau drawer. He would tell me about his day, sanitized for my young ears, in which the knights of law and order always won against the monsters.

On a blustery winter night many years later, a few of his fellow deputies cornered me in a bar and spewed out my old man's sins, from his habit of sleeping on the job to his piss-poor marksmanship. By that time, I had discovered most of the truth about his career on my own, but it required every ounce of my self-control to not break those bastards in half.

When I was in high school, my daddy was terminated by the department for talking back one too many times to his superior officer. But I knew the real reason had everything to do with a gunfight near the reservoir that resulted in the deaths of three cocaine smugglers on a little road trip from Juárez. Actually, "gunfight" is too strong a term. From what I pieced together as an adult, it was more of an execution, and nobody logged any coke into evidence. When the FBI began sniffing around, the cops cut my daddy loose with a warning to keep his mouth shut. Whatever happened to the drugs, I know he never profited from it, because we always had trouble paying our bills.

My daddy was done in law enforcement after that. He took a job as a guard in a new for-profit prison fifty miles north of town, trading in his departmental sidearm for a can of pepper spray and a riot gun loaded with nonlethal plastic buckshot. They assigned him to the lunatic tank, where he spent his shifts in a folding chair in front of the cells, making sure nobody used a sheet or their underwear to hang themselves from the bars. Some nights he had to dodge the shit thrown at him, or call maintenance to deal with a prisoner stuffing their clothes in the toilet.

My daddy's coworkers included an eighteen-year-old kid looking to make a little money before starting college, a drunk with a DUI on his record, and an overweight dude with narcolepsy. All were present on the cell block when a prisoner named Wade Lee Child shoved a sharpened toothbrush into the back of my daddy's neck, but none did more than scream and wave their arms as he bled to death on the concrete.

I spent the next three months in hell, punching anyone who tried to offer their condolences. After that first wave of grief tore through me, I decided to cut a pound of flesh in my daddy's name. I started with his eighteen-year-old colleague, a mouth-breathing moron named Andy, who told me nothing until I broke his nose. Then he admitted to panicking when that lunatic shanked my daddy and running into the prison yard instead of phoning medical. As a reward for his honesty, I only broke Andy's right arm in two places.

But I was minor league compared to my sister. There was no way that Wade Lee Child would ever leave prison a free man, and while he waited for a fresh trial, the administrators—dumbasses all—cycled him back into general population. Frankie became fast friends with a woman whose brother was on the same block, and who had access to a cell phone the prisoners hid in a mattress. In exchange for a hundred bucks to the woman and another fifty to a couple of prison-commissary accounts, Frankie ended up on the line with Wade Lee Child.

The next day at dusk, obeying Frankie's instructions, Child walked to a section of the fence beneath the northwest guard tower, which stood unmanned due to the corporation's cost-cutting measures. Our daddy once told us that the sensors in that section, installed to alert the guards if anyone touched the fence, had burned out long ago. Frankie shared that information with Child, and because the man had an I.Q. roughly equivalent to his shoe size, he never bothered asking the mystery woman on the phone why she wanted him freed.

Child climbed the fence, up and over in five minutes, and disappeared into the miles of scrub that ringed the prison. It would take forty minutes for anyone to notice he was missing, and another five for a guard to trigger the alarm. Child headed in the direction of the setting sun, the brush scraping at his face and plucking at his clothing, humming a mindless tune. If he had kept on that course, he would have been caught within the hour. Instead the guards found nothing except his footprints, and a fresh pair of tire-tracks heading south.

Three nights later, a Burger King manager discovered Child's severed head atop a dumpster behind the restaurant. Someone had smashed out Child's teeth so his mouth could fit a severed piece of his anatomy.

Yeah, Frankie got her pound of flesh, too.

V

"Thank you for saving me," Janine said as I reversed the truck down the driveway. "If I had to spend another five minutes with Susan, I was going to have to tell her the poop story."

Instead of turning right, in the direction of our house, I swung the truck left and hit the gas, anxious to put some distance between us and that demon McMansion. "You should have told her," I laughed, fiddling with the radio. "I would've loved to have seen the look on her face."

"How was the garage?"

"A serious midlife crisis."

"Lord." She gritted her teeth. "Those elitist pricks. When you went into the garage? Susan started talking to me about meth. About how addicts bring it on themselves, and she just couldn't believe how bad it was out here."

"You mention your brother?" After the incident with my AR-15s, Rick had sworn off his beloved drugs and found a job as a line cook at a steakhouse in Boise. I liked to think that Zombie Bill's grisly demise had scared him permanently onto the straight and narrow. I also wondered sometimes if Rick had returned the favor by convincing Janine to start talking, really talking, to me again. Whatever had happened behind the scenes, he would be best man at our remarriage, and I would be happy to have him there.

"No," Janine said. "I just told her it was a real problem here. Then she wanted to talk about vacations to the Caribbean. She suggested we go to some resort in the Dominican Republic. Who the hell are these people?"

"Space aliens," I said. "Or they might as well be."

The radio's seek button landed on a classic rock station blasting Motörhead, which seemed like just the thing for working out some of our tension. Bobbing our heads in sync with the beat, we drove down the two-lane that cut through the black fields, headed for the highway and east.

As the song snarled to a close, we bounced across the railroad tracks that marked the edge of Parma, the town on the fastest route to the highway. A lit sign loomed out of the dark, advertising AMATURE NITE at the local strip club, a gray bunker that offered watery beer, scarred ladies, and, for me, the occasional runaway client downing liquor before his inevitable date with a judge. Every couple of weeks, I gifted the owner, Ricky, a bottle of top-shelf whiskey for allowing me to handcuff people in his parking lot without interference.

Beyond the tracks, we passed a pair of diners that looked like crash-landed UFOs bookending a row of plain brick buildings that served as Parma's main street. No lights in any windows, nobody on the sidewalk. With the exception of the strip club, every local business shut down by nine. In the time it took me to change radio stations, the buildings fell away and the speed limit rose from twenty-five to sixty.

We passed the gas station where the robbery had taken place the other night, its door and pumps webbed with yellow crime-scene tape. Someone had left a bouquet of flowers on the cracked curb. Janine reached over and twisted the radio silent, tapping all the knobs left to right as she did so.

"Hell of a memorial," I said.

"Think the cops will find who did it?"

"Sure. Most criminals are dumb, remember? They'll mess up."

"Remember when we were kids, that convenience store got knocked off over in Eagle, three people killed? My mom wouldn't let me go outside for a week."

I had no memory of that, but nodded anyway.

"You want people to stop feeling safe, kill someone where they buy their gas and potato chips," she said.

When the gas station disappeared from the rearview mirror, Janine cranked the volume on the radio again. The music had transitioned to the news. A hoarse voice shouted about cutting subsidized school lunches, and how that would allow the little tykes to build some much-needed character. I recognized the world-class assholedom of U.S. Senator Ted Ryan, always so determined to rob the poor to fund sweet tax cuts for the rich. As the newscaster cut in, explaining that the honorable gentleman had made those remarks at a press conference in Boise, I switched the radio off.

"It's amazing how our elected representatives give us new reasons to hate them every year," I said.

"I was reading this study," Janine said. "Apparently a lot of Americans think one day they'll be millionaires, so they support those tax cuts for the one percent, because they really believe it'll affect them down the road. I kid you not."

"None of us get to be millionaires."

"We do okay, babe. Mortgage is manageable. I'm up to thirty bucks an hour. Just as long as you don't get your fine ass shot, we'll be okay."

"Right now I'm more worried about cops," I said, nodding at the approaching exit.

We ramped onto the highway. I scanned the medians for police cruisers, half-expecting to see my friend Varney lurking somewhere. Traffic was light and it only took a few minutes to reach the mile-marker where I was pulled over that afternoon.

"Is your stuff there?" Janine asked.

"I'll check," I said. "Stay here."

From the glove compartment I retrieved a small flashlight, clicking it once to test the battery before exiting the truck. Shining the beam into the ditch that separated the eastbound and westbound lanes, I found the crumpled mess of my boat cover and fishing tackle. The impact had bent the bail on one of the reels, and I had lost my favorite lures to the wind, but all told that seemed a small price to pay for having the bulk of my stuff back.

A sedan roared past on the eastbound side, pelting my shoulders with gravel as I scooped up a double-armful of gear. After depositing the load in the back seat of the truck, I slid behind the wheel. "Screw the police," I told Janine.

"Hey," she said. "Maybe he was having a crappy day."

"That's no excuse," I said. "I'm not a criminal. I pay his salary. He should act professional." Glancing in the side mirrors, half-expecting to see a red-and-blue burst of cop lights, I merged into the left lane. "And he mentioned Frankie."

Janine straightened in her seat. "Yeah? What'd he say?"

"That the cops would get her eventually."

"I know you're not going to like me saying this, but maybe that's why he was so angry. Because he recognized the name. It's not like cops show her a lot of love. Or vice versa. You talk to her lately?"

"Not in a couple weeks." Once a month, Frankie and I met for coffee or drinks. The last time, she had asked me to drive north, into the hills, and meet her at the hot spring where we used to play as kids. We lay in the steaming water that gurgled from a fissure in the rock, sharing beers as we talked about what little family we had left. Four of her men sat nearby, rifles balanced on their knees, scanning the steep path that led to the road below. We're just like any other folks, really.

"You know I don't like keeping you from your sister," Janine said, "but she can bring trouble to our doorstep."

"No, she doesn't."

"Oh, sweetie." Janine offered a raised eyebrow as she tapped the dashboard one, two, three, four times, changing fingers with each tap.

"I mean, nothing we haven't dealt with." I stretched in my seat, fighting sleep's soft fingers on my eyelids. If we made it home in twenty minutes, I could score five hours of shut-eye before work. I had good leads on a couple of bail jumpers at the far edge of the valley, nothing too heavy, but you should always be at your perkiest when trying to force people back to jail.

My gut stirred, and a concrete-shattering fart popped through my jeans, filling the cabin with its delicate perfume. I made a show of wrinkling my nose.

Janine's look of disappointment crumbled at the edges.

"That was weak," she said.

"That was strong like bull," I shot back.

"Strong for you maybe, but nothing compared to what I've seen and heard today."

"From what you said, you experienced the apocalypse."

We pulled into our driveway, the floodlight bolted to the roof clicking to life as the truck rumbled past the motion sensor I installed on the corner of the house. My headlights flashed across the dark windows. I sensed something wrong. Nothing seemed out of place—no broken glass, no tools or bikes missing—but nonetheless, a cold weight settled in my stomach.

Janine sensed something. "What?"

"Probably nothing," I said, keeping my voice calm, but Janine knew better. If she had any lingering doubts, I nuked those by opening the glove compartment and removing my pistol.

VI

I wasn't drowsy anymore.

Climbing out of the truck, I held my door open so Janine could crawl out behind me. Easing the door shut as quietly as possible, I backed away from the white light blasting the yard, Janine's hand on my spine as she matched me step for step. We had rehearsed this sort of evasion a few times in broad daylight, always laughing and joking as we did so, and I was proud to see that she carried out her moves seamlessly as a tango partner.

When we reached the short fence that lined our road, I moved us east, skirting the house, angling my body between the windows and Janine. If anyone was inside, they would have seen us pull up, climb out, and retreat into the dark. We crept at barely a walking pace, and it took us a good five minutes to reach the backyard. I ducked us behind the one small tree and paused, listening for sounds, scanning the house for lights or movement. Aside from the buzzing symphony of insects, I heard nothing, saw nothing. Maybe I was too paranoid.

"Stay here," I whispered to Janine. Crouching low, I sprinted for the back door with my pistol raised. The knob twisted freely in my hand, the door opening on blackness. But we had locked it before leaving, right?

Spine pressed to the wall, I inched into the kitchen, pausing at every step to listen for movement. As my night vision adjusted, I saw nothing out of place—drawers closed, wet dishes in the rack, even the small jar of spare change on the counter untouched. Moving faster now, I cleared the living room and headed upstairs, fast through the bedrooms, bathroom, and office before spinning on my heel and returning to the first floor.

Maybe I was too fearful for my own good.

Maybe all those blasts in Iraq had scrambled my brains.

In any case, one last zone to check.

I kneed open the door that led to my special room. No windows meant it was pitch black inside, so I reached over with my free hand and slapped on the lights. As the fluorescents flickered to life, I thought everything was fine. Then I saw the door of the safe ajar. And I always kept that baby shut tight. Didn't I?

I angled toward the safe, gripped the edge of the door, and pulled it open.

On the floor of the safe crouched a naked girl, her bloodless body pressed tight against my long guns. I leapt back, heart racing. Her half-lidded pupils stared through me, her gray lips open in a frozen snarl. She was dead. It was hard to tell from all the bruises and cuts on her face, but she wasn't older than sixteen; it was a deep safe but only someone small could fit inside it and still pull the door almost closed.

Praying that Janine would stay outside for a few minutes longer, I holstered my pistol and bent down, careful not to touch anything. I observed the feet, caked with dirt, the toes riddled with broken blisters, the nails split. A red line scored the right ankle, as if someone had bound it with rope or a cuff. There was a small hole an inch below her ribs, crusted with dark blood. Maybe from a .22.

Never taking my eyes from the body, I stood and fished my phone from my pocket. I snapped photos of the dead girl's face, arms, legs, torso. There was a little tattoo on her right forearm, a curvy symbol I didn't recognize, professionally done. Walking backward, I examined the rug, evaluating stains. It was hard to spot the dried blood against the dark fibers, but once I locked on the trail, I followed it through the kitchen and out the back door, snapping photos as I went.

"Sweetie?"

Janine stood in the grass, her hands bunched against her chest, her face a mask of worry in the moonlight.

"It's okay," I said, although everything was not okay. "Just stay there."

"Why? What's up?"

"Bit of a situation inside the house," I said, lifting my phone and dialing the cops. "Nothing we can't handle, okay?"

"What happened?" The dismay in her voice threatened to rip my heart out. We had spent too long creating this new place for us, away from the fire and ruin that had defined so many years of our lives. And now one bled-out tweaker threatened to shatter that illusion for good. Why couldn't this girl have died in some random field instead of my house?

Why had she crawled in there in the first place?

VII

The cops appeared half an hour later. Before they arrived, I swept through the first floor in case I had left out anything I didn't want John Q. Law to see. After giving myself the all clear, I phoned my lawyer and told him to hustle his ass over, per hour be damned.

Next I brought Janine into the kitchen, where she took a seat at the counter, her head in her hands. Stepping into the driveway, I phoned Frankie.

"You in a safe place to talk?" My sister and I carried phones with a custom Android operating system that offered added encryption, so we could chat without fear of anyone listening in. Frankie had purchased the devices for us after the incident with Zombie Bill at the quarry. When you fire a rocket or two on American soil, the feds start showing a keen interest in your business activities.

"Depends on how you define 'safe,'" she laughed. "I sleep with danger."

"I don't want to hear about your weird-ass sex life." Usually I would spend a good ten minutes joking with my sister, but I was in no mood tonight. "I got a dead body in my house."

That stopped her chuckling. "Anyone we know?"

"No," I said. "Looks like a girl, teenager, naked,

stuffed in my gun safe. You hear anything?"

"You think it's a setup?"

"No, I think she got in there herself. We were at a party. One of us must have forgotten to lock the back before we left."

"You forget to lock the safe, too?"

"I must have," I said. "I had so many things on my mind, I think I closed it and forgot to throw the handle."

"This is where I make a joke about you and gun safety."

"Please don't. You know I'm usually good about it. I got a kid around."

"Okay. Why anyone would want to die in your gun safe is beyond me." Over the phone, I heard papers rustling, a glass tinkling. "Now you've got me out of bed. You want me to head out there, help with disposal? I'll call the Monkey Man. He's got a whole new kit, chainsaw and everything."

"No," I said. "I called the cops."

"What?"

"Sorry, did I start speaking Arabic? I phoned the police. And my lawyer."

"You straight-edge bastard. Should have let me handle it. I'm so much cleaner."

I suspected she was right. A chainsaw and a couple of garbage bags are pretty good tools for dealing with life's little problems. And the idea of cops in my house scared the crap out of me, especially after the incident with Varney. "You know I'm trying to stay on the straight and narrow these days," I said. "But if you want to help, keep your ear to the ground."

"Janine see it?"

"No, and she's not going to."

"Ugh. Whatever it is, it'll be okay. How many gunfights have we been in, between the two of us? Compared to that, everything else is easy."

If she was trying to calm me down, it worked. "That's a good way of looking at it," I said. "I'll call you back in a bit, okay?"

"Stay frosty," she said, and hung up.

A minute later, a cruiser swept into my driveway with a single siren-beep. I recognized neither of the two cops who climbed out, young boys who looked barely old enough to shave their upper lips. They seemed nervous as I escorted them into the house.

Janine nodded to the officers when they stated their names. I pointed toward my safe room, following closely as they ducked through the door. "If you got to vomit," I said, "make sure you do it outside. I already need to get that rug cleaned."

While one of them snapped on a pair of latex gloves and eased open the safe's door, the other stood a few feet away with his hand on his holstered pistol. I made a point of standing in their field of view, my hands in sight, as I calculated times in my head. If he drove at lunatic speeds, it would take our lawyer another twenty minutes or so to reach our house from his fabulous apartment in downtown Boise. In the meantime, I intended to keep my mouth shut.

Imagine my surprise when, after ten minutes of fidgeting in the kitchen, I heard a fine-tuned roar outside. I stepped out the front door in time to catch the yellow blur of a Porsche rocketing past. Two hundred yards later, its brake-lights flared, accompanied by the screech of brakes.

Rather than turn around on the narrow road, my lawyer set the Porsche in reverse and slammed the gas, nearly colliding on the return trip with the medical examiner's van turning into the driveway. A big black sedan trailed the van, its front seats filled by a pair of big men in off-the-rack suits: detectives, irate.

"It's just my attorney," I shouted at the growing crew of law enforcement.

The Porsche veered onto the shoulder and stopped, missing my mailbox by inches.

Whatever image those police had of a lawyer, Johnny certainly did not fit that ideal. At this late hour, called un-expectedly by a client to whom he owed a large and bloody favor, he wore a crumpled dress shirt along with a pair of musty jeans. At least the shirt hid the enormous skull tattoo on his back, and his pupils seemed clear. Be-tween college and law school, Johnny had picked up a bad cocaine habit he never shook.

"You okay?" he asked as he stumbled across the yard, his forehead slick with sweat. "You say anything?"

"Just that I found a body," I said. "Nothing other than that."

"Good." He headed inside, gesturing for me to follow.

After hugging Janine, Johnny helped himself to a glass of water from the kitchen sink and sat in one of the stools at the counter, alternating between watching the cops work and checking his phone. Inside the safe room, two crime-scene techs set up camp, snapping photographs every few seconds as they examined the body. The chief medical examiner swept past us, a clipboard in her hand.

The two detectives seemed nice at first, but a smiling cop is still a hair-trigger away from arresting you for murder. The senior one, Harry, was a swarthy hulk with a soggy cigar clenched in his jaw. It made him resemble a bulldog with a stick. The other one, a reedy guy with a pasty face, introduced himself as Bob.

"You're Frankie's brother?" Harry asked as we took seats at the kitchen table, nodding to Bob. An entire conversation about my family in one glance. They scanned me for the usual sweats and tics of guilt. I stared back at them with my blankest expression, trying to ignore my own slamming heart.

"My client's relations have nothing to do with this," Johnny said. "Before we start, we need to set some ground rules here. My client is concerned by what happened here, obviously, and he's more than happy to help out in any way necessary. But bringing in his family is not going to help things."

"Is this why you called a lawyer?" Bob said. "To dick around with us?"

"Seemed prudent," I said. Unlike most civilians, I've spent my life dealing with law enforcement. Cops will always tell you that having a lawyer present makes you look guilty, that they just want a friendly chat. Pro tip: it is never a friendly chat, especially with a body in the next room.

"That's a mighty big word, 'prudent,'" Bob said.

"I read a lot."

"You know the dead woman in the other room?" Harry asked.

"No," I said. "Never seen her before."

Bob pointed at Janine, who had taken a seat on the couch in the living room, her hands torturing the air out of her stress ball. "Your wife know her?"

I shook my head. "No."

Harry chomped his wet mess of a cigar. "So how did she get into your house?"

"We don't know," I said. "Maybe we left the back door unlocked."

"You leave your gun safe unlocked, too?" Bob asked.

"Not usually," I said. "But we were in a rush, going out. My daughter's away, so maybe I was a little too relaxed about it."

It was Harry's turn to pop a question: "Why was she in the safe?"

"You tell me."

"Looked like she was shot," Bob said. "Were you home all night?"

I shook my head again.

Bob sighed. "How about you tell us about your where-abouts?"

I glanced at Johnny, who nodded, and I filled them in on everything: our drinks with the neighbors, the trip down the highway to retrieve our stuff, the return home. When I finished, the detectives traded a look of brewing frustration. But what did they expect? That I would admit to murdering a random woman, dumping her in my safe, and calling the cops?

"We'll have to talk to those neighbors," Harry said.

"Of course," Johnny said. "We'll give you their names and address."

"And we'll know more once the medical examiner settles on a time of death," Bob said. "It's convenient that you weren't here, right? When a woman died on your property?"

I looked at Johnny, who said: "It's neither convenient nor inconvenient. It's just what is."

"Is your wife worried?" Harry asked.

"She's not mute. Why don't you ask her?"

Harry laughed, a sound without joy. "Girl dies on your

property, killer's maybe out there. You don't seem too worried about that at all."

Johnny raised a hand, about to shut down that line of inquiry, when I touched his wrist. "I am worried," I said. "And my wife is worried. But freaking out isn't going to solve this situation. As for security, we can handle ourselves around here."

"Who's your next-door neighbor?" Bob asked.

"Name of Luke Jameson. Veteran, he keeps to himself. Good guy. I don't think he has anything to do with this."

"You don't think," Bob snorted.

"My client's been compliant," Johnny said. "You have no right to use that tone."

"We'll use any tone we want, counselor," Harry said, pounding the table. "Your client has a dead body in his house. In my experience, when you find a body in a house, the house's owner generally had something to do with it. And if not him, someone nearby."

"Maybe that's what someone wants you to think," I said, unable to help myself.

Bob tilted his head. "We'll see. How many guns do you own?"

"Everything in the safe," I said, neglecting to mention the 9mm in the Bible in the truck. I wanted one pistol in reserve in case the cops confiscated the rest.

The detectives exchanged a look.

"None of them's a murder weapon, if that's what you're getting at." Of the pistols in the safe, the .45 had a little too much play in the slide, but I liked how the .38 felt on the range. I felt nostalgic for both firearms even before the police tagged and bagged them. Weapons in the system have a nasty way of disappearing.

"You'll need a warrant," Johnny said.

Bob widened his eyes in mock horror. "We have so much probable cause, it's unbelievable. We're going to seize, okay? You'll get them back after we test. If you're innocent, surely you won't have a problem with that, right?"

I nodded at Johnny, who sighed and ran his hands through his hair. The detectives stood without another word and entered the safe room. I balled my hands and squeezed until the tendons in my forearms ached, which vented some of my anger. Having combed his scalp into a sweat-shiny tangle, Johnny stood, almost colliding with Janine as she went out the back door.

"Janine..." I said.

But my wife disappeared into the dark. Raising a finger for Johnny to wait, I exited the house and followed her across the yard to the fence, where she tossed her stress ball into the grass and stood with her back to me, arms crossed over her chest, haloed by the faint stars.

"We can stay somewhere else tonight," I told her. "Your sister's or something."

She shook her head. "This is so messed up. What if the kid had been with us?"

I flashed on Scott Parson on the pavement, wheezing, his cheeks streaked with tears. How do you defend your child against the worst of the world? Thinking about it made my stomach cramp. "We'll figure out what happened."

She snorted. "That's what you always say."

If it had been anyone else, I might have grabbed her elbow and spun her around, forced a conversation face-to-face. But this was my wife, and my anger at the cops had cooled to ash. "Usually we don't have dead bodies in the house, dear," I said.

"No, I meant your problem-solving mode. Where you say we'll always get through whatever." She raised her face to the sky and sighed. "Like you won't let yourself acknowledge how bad something is."

"I do know how bad this is," I said. "That's why I'm in problem-solving mode."

"Some problems can't be solved," she said. "And they're too big to forget."

I placed a hand on Janine's shoulder and squeezed. She shifted her hand to cover mine and pressed back.

An hour later, the medical examiner's van conveyed the girl's body into the night, trailed by the cruiser and the detectives' unmarked sedan, which had my pistols, rifle, and shotguns in the trunk. At least when Zombie Bill had taken my AR-15s, I had a fifty-fifty chance of seeing them again.

Johnny stuck around for a few more minutes to offer the usual boilerplate about not speaking to anybody about the murder without calling him first, but I had a hard time paying attention. I kept glancing at Janine, who had returned from the backyard to sit on the couch, as far away from the safe room as possible while remaining inside the house. I wondered how long it would take for everything to return to normal. If anything could return to normal.

I had forgotten to tell the cops about finding that silver necklace near the fence. It was still in my safe, where it would remain the least of my problems for the time being. What an awful fucking day.

VIII

When your sister sells illegal weapons for a living, and uses one of those weapons to blast a rival into barbeque, setting up a coffee meet requires old-fashioned spycraft. First you spend an hour driving randomly through downtown Boise to make sure you lose any unmarked cars full of cops or feds. Next you pull into the three-story parking garage near the hospital, to prevent anyone from seeing you duck into a van with tinted windows driven by one of your sister's tougher-looking dudes, who drives you west, out of the city.

For today's location, Frankie had decided to indulge her love of truck pulls. After forty minutes on the highway, we pulled into the gravel lot behind a dirt racetrack, growling past a row of booths where charming kids in scout uniforms sold cookies and lemonade. We bypassed the regular parking slots and stopped behind the wooden bleachers, out of sight of the main road. The bleachers were packed with people drinking beer and smoking cigarettes as they waited for the vehicular mayhem to begin.

"Lot of witnesses," I told the driver, looking around.

"She's up in the, what you call it, that wood thing," he said, pointing through the windshield at the announcer's booth at the top of the bleachers. It was a plywood box where a couple of volunteers would narrate the action at two hundred words a minute, sweltering in the dust and heat but keeping dehydration at bay with massive quantities of alcohol.

"Got it," I said, and exited the vehicle alone. I bought a ticket at the booth, along with a box of Thin Mints from one of the girl scouts. It was my first meal since our fish dinner the previous night, and with my adrenaline fading, I needed a sugar rush to keep me upright.

I paused in my climb up the bleachers to the announcer's booth, chewing my first four cookies and admiring the track. Half of southern Idaho's gearheads had turned out for this one: a motley collection of amped-up trucks lined the center oval, bodies bristling with chromed exhaust pipes and massive, weighted bumpers. The drivers sat in lawn chairs beside their mighty mechanical steeds, chugging from cans and waiting for the festivities to begin.

I walked into the announcer's booth, which reminded me too much of the temporary cells we used for prisoners on Iraqi bases. The announcer, a ruffian with a gray goatee and wild hair, sat at a card table beside the wide cutout that served as a window, a microphone in his hand. Frankie sat beside him, dressed despite the heat in her usual uniform of black cargo pants and a black long-sleeve shirt.

Reaching into the cooler beside her chair, she retrieved a beer and tossed it to me underhand. Stuffing my box of cookies in my armpit, I caught it and popped the tab in one easy motion.

"You've had a hell of a week, bro," she said as I plopped down in a rickety folding chair beside her.

"Been through worse," I said, truthfully. Once you've survived for three days in a wrecked building surrounded by insurgent snipers, with no water and a single bucket as a toilet for thirty soldiers, everything else seems easy by comparison. "Where's your security?"

"Brought my favorite pyromaniac," Frankie said with a note of pride in her voice, pointing out the window at the far side of the track, where the van that brought me had parked beneath the rusted-out scoreboard. My driver sat on the bumper, the Monkey Man beside him. That plastic chimpanzee mask might have stood out in other circumstances, but nobody seemed to notice it amid the dust, revving engines, and giant flags.

"We okay to talk?" I said, nodding toward the announcer, who stared at the track like a monk trying to glimpse God.

"Sure, Joe here's busy," Frankie said, gesturing for me to hand over the cookies. "Besides, he owes me a favor, right, Joe?"

"Focused on this," Joe muttered. On the track, a trio of workers prepared the massive steel sled for the first pull. I had attended enough of these events to know I was about to witness an awe-inspiring contest between tons of deadweight and the most powerful internal-combustion engines this side of a passenger jet. Once a truck was hooked to the sled, the driver would try to drag it as far as possible down the track; a series of gears on the sled, meanwhile, would slowly move an enormous weight forward from the rear axles, making it harder to pull with each passing second.

"I got some money on this one," Frankie said, popping a cookie in her mouth. "Cops giving you too much shit over that body?"

"Not yet," I said, chugging my brew. "But you know they'll make me swing by, answer more questions. Johnny was a star, by the way."

"He'd better be. We buried that problem for him."

"So to speak. With the cops, I was shocked they didn't bring you up. Maybe they're waiting for next interview."

"Ever since our little thing with Zombie Bill, I've had some big heat on me," she said, eating another three cookies. At this rate, she would finish the box before the first truck pulled its load. "This time around, like, FBI. That's why we do the thing with the cars to get you here. But the local cops? You know those rednecks don't worry me too much. They can shove their questions right up their doughnut-stuffed asses."

"We're rednecks."

"No, we're not. I don't act like one. You only pretend to act like one."

"What do you mean?"

"You're smart, bro. Maybe smarter than I am, and I'm pretty damn smart. You use big words, and you read all of your wife's books once she's done with them. But you hide that big brain behind your stupid T-shirts and your tattoos and this 'aw shucks' attitude. It might fool most people, but not me, no, sir."

"If I was smart, I'd be a hell of a lot richer."

"You could get into business with me. Make a ton of money."

Beside us, Joe pattered into the microphone. Like an engine on a cold day, he started slow, but as the workers hitched the first truck to the sled, and the truck's after-market pipes belched clouds of black smoke, his speech became a torrent. He complimented the fine weather for this sporting event, praised the audience and the Good Lord and the nation's armed forces, diverted for a bit into the history of sled pulls, veered back into a description of this particular driver's wins and losses, and concluded by taking a deep breath and inviting everyone to watch the show.

Frankie scooted her chair for a better view of the track.

"I may have a couple hundred in my bank account," I told the back of her head, "but I told you before: not my style."

She waved her hand. "Your loss. Being a criminal is a real thrill, is what they never tell you in school."

The truck roared, its front wheels almost rising off the track as it powered forward in a cloud of dust and oily smoke, the audience screaming, the sled hissing as it fought momentum, the weight on its back ratcheting sure and slow as doom. Despite the driver pushing the gas pedal to the floor, the truck began to slow, its roar rising to a thinner shriek that matched the pitch of the crowd. After fifty yards, the battle was over, and the driver shut down his engine before it blew.

"Weak," Frankie snorted. "I just lost twenty bucks."

When we were kids, Frankie earned money by selling oregano to middle schoolers, telling them it was pot, and using the money to purchase heavy metal albums. (Our mother always wondered why her spices seemed to disappear so quickly.) One of those little tykes ratted on her, of course, earning her a month-long suspension. The following night, our school principal's station wagon exploded in his driveway, injuring nobody but burning down his garage. What a funny coincidence.

By the time Frankie graduated college—the only member of our family to do so—she had upgraded her business from fake weed to real guns. For five years, she bought secondhand weapons on the cheap from scary guys in Montana and Oregon, then drove the arsenals down to Mexico by herself. It was a good retail operation, and once she built enough of a reputation, she decided to go wholesale. Now she ran the equivalent of Amazon.com for murder machines.

Yes, I hated what she did for a living.

No, I would never turn her in.

The track crew unhitched the sled, and the driver tried restarting his pickup. The engine coughed and sputtered and died. A tow truck motored into view. While the audience waited for the track to clear, and Joe filled the air with nonsense about potatoes and patriotism, I pulled out my phone and flicked it to life. Tilting the screen so Frankie could see photos of last night's corpse, I asked: "Recognize her?"

With the back of her hand, Frankie wiped crumbs from her lips. "I don't. Should I?"

I swiped to a close-up of the girl's tattoo. "You recognize the ink? The symbol?"

"Doesn't ring any bells."

"I don't know, sis, I'm grasping at straws here."

Frankie returned my box of cookies and sipped her beer. I tried reading her mind through her eyes. "I'm sorry, bro," she finally said. "What this whole thing looks like to me? I think it's pretty straightforward. Girl running from someone, sees a house, finds it unlocked, tries to hide, dies from wounds."

Leaning my chair against the wall, I mulled that possibility. It might have been a hundred degrees inside the booth, yet my skin felt cold. "There was a piece of jewelry in my yard, right by the fence line. I found it a little while before we left. Maybe it was hers, if she was hiding in that field. You know I don't cut the grass back there."

"Sounds weird. If she's hurt, why would she hide out? Why not cry for help?"

"Good point," I said. "So let's put the jewelry aside for the time being, say it has nothing to do with her. If she was being chased, wouldn't that person have come into the house, finished the job? Why risk her finding a phone, calling the cops?"

"Maybe they lost her track, and they weren't going to start kicking down doors looking for her. Number of guns in Idaho, it's a risky thing to invade someone's property."

"True."

"I know you probably don't want to hear it, but you should think about whether someone really is trying to frame you, or send a message. They come in, dump the body, leave."

I snorted. "If this is a frame, it's a real long list of suspects. I've sent hundreds of people back to jail."

"Outside of work, you piss anyone off lately?"

"I made a cop angry the other day."

She straightened in her seat. "Cop?"

"I was driving back from the lake. He pulled me over because the cover flew off the boat. Seemed upset. Screaming, yelling, everything."

"If someone was going to mess with you, a cop would be bad news. What was this pig's name?"

"Varney. Didn't catch his first name. But that should be enough, right? How many people have a weirdo last name like that?"

"I'll look into it. And forward me those photos on your phone. I'll put out the word, see what comes back. Might get lucky on the tattoo."

The tow truck had cleared the first victim off the track. The second contender raced his engine as the crew finished hooking up the sled. This pickup featured screaming-eagle decals on its doors, along with a riot of American flag stickers on its front bumper. Joe cleared his throat, bent to the microphone, and encouraged the audience to cheer its lungs out.

"Thank you. How's everything else?" I asked, rushing the words before I lost Frankie to the next pull.

"Wishing we'd used regular bullets on Zombie Bill." Frankie swallowed the last of her beer and opened a fresh can. Hellish temperatures or no, her forehead remained dry, her cheeks unflushed. The heat never gets to my little ice queen.

"We'll survive," I said.

"Thanks for your optimism." She smirked. "You know my shipping container? Got raided. Luckily I wasn't there. Not like I don't have other places to crash, but I liked that one in particular."

"Your other houses are better."

"Indeed. If I didn't have an army and a lot of guns, I'd actually be worried."

The second truck roared its engine and pulled for glory, making it seventy yards before black smoke puffed from its pipes and it wheezed to a stop. The sled was conquering all comers today. I stood, leaving the box of cookies on my seat.

"Going already?" Frankie asked.

"Yeah," I said. "Got to get back to work. But keep the cookies. My treat."

"I ate most of them, anyway."

"I knew you would. Love you, sis."

Frankie's man seemed upset at having to leave the pull early, until I offered to buy him lunch at a drive-through on the way home. We ate our burgers and drank our milkshakes in silence on the trip back to Boise, where he dropped me at the parking garage. How Frankie became so good at being bad was a mystery beyond my comprehension. And despite my issues over her choice of profession, I always liked the idea of a sibling capable of blasting off someone's head at two hundred yards.

Speaking of weapons, I made the tactical decision to leave my 9mm locked in my glove compartment when I went back to work. The idea of chasing after deadbeats without my pistol on my hip made me a little nervous, but so did the idea of a cop seeing me armed. News of the body in my house had no doubt spread along the secret nervous system that linked police and criminals in the valley. An officer or detective who saw me with a filled holster might start asking questions, maybe attempt to add the firearm to my arsenal already in lockup.

Instead I took a tip from my old friend Rooster Marley and stopped off at a sporting-goods store to purchase a wooden baseball bat. "Got any barbed wire I can wrap around this?" I asked the kid behind the register. "I was thinking of going full Negan." I failed to make him laugh.

What a week.

After knocking on some doors—and failing to nail any deadbeats—I drove to our temporary home at the Belle Rive, a boutique hotel on Main Street. What was once a standard-issue motor lodge now offered tasteful lighting, steel and dark-wood highlights, and a hipster eatery where the parking lot had been. The rooms included retro furniture on spindly legs, inoffensive abstract art, and showers with water pressure powerful enough to cut through steel. Although it was expensive to stay there, I figured it would only be a few days, and the funkiness appealed to my wife. In typical Janine fashion, she had brought ten paperback books in her duffel bag, and only two extra pairs of underwear.

I entered our room on the second floor to find her sitting by the window in the one soft chair, laptop open and pecking away at work. I kissed her on the forehead and placed my pistol and holster on the nightstand before moving to the sideboard, where we had three grocery bags of supplies, mostly snacks and alcohol. "How're you doing?" I asked, popping the cork on the whiskey and pouring a quarter-inch into a disposable plastic cup.

"How do you think?" she asked, flat.

"I saw Frankie," I said. "She's going to help out."

Janine kept typing. Her job let her work remotely, a great perk for anyone forced to flee their home. Lord knows we needed her paycheck.

"Come on," I said. "Just talk to me."

"You're drinking whiskey," she said, never looking up from her screen.

"I know," I said. "Takes the edge off."

"I thought you quit hard liquor."

I paused with the cup halfway to my lips. "I'm not an alcoholic."

"You had a lot of wine and beer the other night. I'm surprised I let you drive. Stupid me."

I placed the cup back on the sideboard. "Come on," I said. "Just talk to me. You know I can't deal with this passive-aggressive crap."

"Nothing passive about it, sweetie." Her eyes met mine, blue and cold as a glacier. "When we got back together, and you started talking marriage again, you made me a promise. It wasn't a big promise but it was important to me. Remember what it was?"

I looked away. On the sideboard beside the grocery bags, Janine had lined her books in a neat row, from tallest spine to shortest. Dashiell Hammett's *Nightmare Town* was the nearest title. How perfect. "That I wouldn't bring my work home," I said.

"That's right. And you broke that promise."

"What do you mean?" I took a step toward her. "Are you talking about the girl in the safe? What the hell does that have to do with my work?"

"Everything," she said, slapping the laptop closed. "Normal people with normal jobs, you think things like that happen to them?"

"This wasn't my fault," I said, my voice rising. "I got no idea why that girl was there. I have no idea who she was."

"And now Frankie's involved."

"I'm not going to turn down my sister's help."

"No, no, I'm sorry, but your sister's a problem. You think those cops took all your guns because they think you killed that girl? Um, no. They did it because you're her brother." She puffed out her cheeks and loosed a long, theatrical sigh. "They're punishing us because she's an arms dealer."

"She's also family. And a huge help."

"Not as helpful as you think." Janine tossed her laptop on the bed and rose to me, so close I felt her warm breath on my chin. I had the absurd urge to kiss her, hard. That tactic had stopped some of our fights in the past. Reading my mind, she placed a hand against my chest and stepped back until her elbow locked, keeping me at bay.

"I have a low tolerance for hotels," she said. "I need my own space, my own bed. And so does our little girl, once she comes home. So you need to go out there and make sure we're safe, okay? I don't want us to have to go to my mother's."

And there it was, the threat. To say that I had a bad relationship with Janine's mother Sarah was like saying that World War II had been a little squabble over real estate. When I married her daughter the first time around, Sarah had shown up to City Hall in a long black dress, like a widow on the way to a funeral, and spent the ten-minute ceremony bawling into a tissue. Things had only gone downhill from there.

"Okay," I said, gently taking Janine's hand from my chest. "I'm doing my best. It's my house, too. We'll be back there before you know it."

"We'd better," she said.

IX

In the restaurant outside, I took a seat at an empty table and, after lingering too long over the hard-liquor options on the menu, ordered a coffee. I sipped it slowly as I watched the hipsters at the next table giggling over chocolate cake. I hoped against hope that Janine would come downstairs and break me out of this funk, but it was my ringing phone that interrupted my thoughts.

Answering, I heard an unfamiliar voice on the other end of the line. "Is this safe?" he asked.

"Sure," I said. "I don't bite."

"You asked about a tattoo?"

It was one of Frankie's people. I waved for the waitress and made a scribbling gesture with my free hand. Wrinkling her nose at me, she handed over a red ballpoint as I flattened out a paper napkin. "Yes, that's right," I said. "What do you got?"

"It's a logo from a wine bottle," the voice said. "Raven Creek Winery, down on the Snake River."

"You're shitting me."

"I never kid," the voice said. It was hard to tell if he was kidding. "Don't think ill of the dead. I guess she thought it looked nice."

"You got a name for her?"

"I'm getting to that. The tattoo was done at Flaming Ink, you know it?"

"Yeah." It was a small parlor a few blocks from my hotel, with a quartet of adjustable tattoo chairs and black walls covered with framed photographs of client ink. The owner, Mad Mel, had needled every inch of his body with elaborate designs, including his face. He was a good guy in my book, by which I mean he always accepted my twenties and forties in exchange for information.

"She got it maybe six months ago," the man said. "Her name was Ruth Jenner, twenty years old."

"Got a last known address?"

"Happy Trails Trailer Park, slot twelve. Lived with her mother and sister. That's from public records. If you're going to ask my name, I'm going to tell you to screw off, but it's not personal, okay?"

"Okay?" I said.

The man chuckled and hung up.

I needed to give Janine more time before trying to reengage. Steering onto the highway, I turned the radio to a channel of angry guitars, hoping the sonic chaos would soothe my nerves a little. As much as Janine and I tried to live normal lives together, we had never settled into that comfort zone that so many other couples seemed to have, where the biggest concern was the mortgage or the car payment. It had led to our first divorce. I thought back to our rich neighbors with their ugly house and beautiful car in the garage, and I envied their boring lives.

I turned off at the correct exit, into an anonymous neighborhood of strip malls and dead fields. Tucked behind a sagging chain-link fence, the Happy Trails Trailer Park looked pretty unhappy: row upon row of double-wides with grimy windows and dented walls lit a sickly yellow by the few streetlights that seemed to work. Cruising through the front gate, I passed an old witch sitting in a fold-out chair on the sidewalk, puffing on a hand-rolled cigarette. She raised a flabby arm stained blue with ancient tattoos and offered me a tall middle finger. I gave her a hearty thumbs-up and kept driving.

I found slot twelve on the far side of the park, tight against the fence and hidden from view by a low concrete wall that must have once served a purpose but now seemed to exist solely as a canvas for graffiti. As I parked on the far side of the wall and climbed out, I saw a couple of buckets tossed on the gravel outside the trailer.

Through the open doorway of the trailer stepped a huge, shirtless Viking with SS lightning bolts inked on his neck. He clutched a black garbage bag in one work-gloved hand, a short axe in the other. The guy obviously not doing your ordinary cleanup, even before my nose caught the wet-pennies smell of fresh meat.

Our eyes met, and we knew the score. His grip shifted on the ax.

On reflex, my hand dipped for my holster—and touched belt.

I had left my pistol in the truck's glove compartment.

Fuckity fuck. Of all the fucking days not to carry.

The Viking dropped the garbage bag—it slapped wetly on the gravel—and strode toward me, moving with enough speed to prevent me from making it to my truck in time. As he closed in, I saw his thick torso smeared with drying blood.

Glancing around for any sort of weapon, I spied a Sharpie pen at the base of the retaining wall, no doubt thrown by the same kid who had tried to write a jagged SUX DIX on the concrete.

Scooping low, I grabbed the Sharpie and retreated toward my truck, holding the pen in my fist so the plastic cap poked out. I knew from personal experience that it hurts like hell to have that hard bit jammed in your soft spots. But a Sharpie can do little against an axe wielded by a Viking with a couple hundred pounds of muscle and a headful of meth and bad ideas.

"This ain't your day," the Viking said in a surprisingly high-pitched voice.

I said nothing in return, only gritted my jaw and raised my fists.

When he came within range, he swung the axe in a tight upward arc, intending to gut me from the get-go. I saw it coming and sidestepped, the steel missing my arm by inches. I threw a straight punch to his chest, driving the tip of the Sharpie between his ribs. He winced and sucked air between his teeth.

I stepped close, inside the radius of his swing, and aimed for his right eye. If the Sharpie cut his eyebrow or forehead, the blood might blind him. Before I could hit him, he slammed an elbow into my forearm, and my numbed fingers dropped the pen.

I stumbled back a step, and he swung the axe overhead. I kicked him in the side of the left knee. He buckled, the weapon wobbling from his grasp, his mouth cracked open in pain.

Fighters usually have bad knees. Remember that the next time you find yourself in a vicious brawl with a neo-Nazi.

I kicked him again, this time in the face. He flopped onto

his back, blood pouring from his nose, and I kicked him a third time in the back of the head. I was taking no chances. I planted a final boot in his ribs—just to make sure he wasn't faking—before trotting back to my truck, where I retrieved my pistol and a pair of handcuffs from the glove compartment.

After I had my new friend cuffed and trussed on the curb in front of the trailer, I took a few minutes to breathe. A tingling life had returned to my right hand, and my foot ached from slamming it against hard bone. Aside from that, I seemed in pretty fine shape for surviving an axe fight. I cursed myself for leaving the pistol in my truck. Never break your own rules—

From deep in the gloom, I heard the scrape of feet on gravel. Hand on pistol, I scanned until I spotted a citizen in front of a double-wide maybe fifty feet away. He wore a red baseball cap and a wifebeater T-shirt, and held a phone to his ear. Calling the police, I hoped.

I waved and headed for the bag that the Viking had dropped before the fight. From its crimped mouth came a stench of blood so strong it made my nostrils twinge. I paced a circle around it, noting how it bulged liquidly, and figured the cops could handle whatever was inside.

Nobody had left the trailer during our fight, so I assumed the Viking was alone. Nonetheless I had my pistol raised as I headed up the front stairs, steeling myself for the worst.

I did two tours in Iraq, including a weeklong stint in Fallujah as that city descended into an orgy of burning bodies and chaos. Some of my friends dealt with the horror by growing hard shells, but I never developed that sort of armor. When I saw something awful, I felt it. So in the doorway of the trailer I hesitated, drawing several deep breaths.

I knew nobody inside was alive.

The doorway opened onto a small kitchen, its counter, sink, and cabinets painted with blood and bits of raw meat. On the floor below the sink, in a plastic bucket, I saw garbage bags and a jumbo bottle of bleach, along with sponges and a roll of paper towels. My friend outside had wiped some of the bloody tiles pink, but his cleanup job had hardly begun.

Lucky me.

I took a single step onto a clean tile, to better study the photographs clipped to the fridge door. I recognized Ruth Jenner in the largest one, vibrant and smiling in a field, her arm wrapped around a stocky teenage boy in a football uniform. She looked clean and fresh, her whole life an open field ahead of her. She had that silver pendant around her neck. The boy's face seemed familiar, but I couldn't quite place it. The part of my brain not stunned by this slaughterhouse made a mental note to investigate that further.

A wide red smear led from the kitchen down a short hallway. I took a big enough step in that direction to glimpse the bathroom stall at the far end, splattered in blood. The shower curtain, torn from the rod, covered a pile of leaking flesh.

I was lucky. If I had shown up at the house an hour earlier, I might have run into a neo-Nazi assault team, tricked out with bullet-resistant vests and surgical gloves and enough blades and pistols to butcher a herd of rhinos. I know how these things go.

The cold night air smacked my face as I left the trailer,

startling me back to reality. I took a lungful of fresh air and held it, willing my heart to slow its gallop. Once I felt a little calmer, I approached the cuffed Viking. Awake now, facedown and thrashing, he cursed and spat blood on the gravel.

"Who was in there?" I asked. "Ruth Jenner's family? What did you do, you son of a bitch?"

"Pig," the Viking said.

"I'm no cop," I said. "Let me ask you again: what happened in there?"

The Viking kept his silence. I heard sirens in the distance and stepped away from my prisoner. I wanted to return the pistol to my glove compartment before the law appeared.

When the first two cops arrived, they handcuffed me and took my pistol until they figured out the situation, although they were smart enough to plop me on the curb a fair distance from the Viking. They entered the trailer shouting like a pair of action-movie bros. A minute later they emerged with tight faces and downcast gazes, silent until one of them called in a homicide.

Harry the Detective arrived in record time. "What a co-incidence," he said, once the cops had placed the Viking in the back of a cruiser and uncuffed me.

Rubbing my wrists, I stepped aside to avoid a cop running yellow tape around the perimeter. "Trailer was where that dead girl lived," I said. "The one we found in my house. Her name is Ruth Jenner."

"How you know that?" Harry asked.

"I got a call," I said. "I don't know who, but the guy gave me her name."

"You get that sort of thing a lot?" Harry asked. "Mys-terious benefactors, calling you out of the blue, giving you information?"

"Sure," I said. "Part of my profession. Folks are always calling me, telling me where to find other folks so I can drag them back to jail, whatever. I'm just a pawn getting played. I can't tell you anything other than that."

"Sounds like a crap life," Harry said.

"As long as I get paid in the end. I'm going to need my pistol back."

"This is a crime scene," he said, in the dull voice of a seasoned bureaucrat.

"Stop messing with me," I said. "Bodies inside are cut up. Nobody heard any shots. You take this gun, and I guarantee my lawyer is going to call up the NRA, and they will stuff enough lawyers up your ass to open a firm in there."

I sounded dangerously close to whining, but the legal threat seemed to fix something in Harry's head. He stepped back and nodded at the Viking's shadowy hulk in the back seat of the cruiser. "A couple years back, I had an informant, buried deep with the Aryan Brotherhood. Someone leaked his name. I spent an hour on the phone calling in everything short of the Marines to save this guy and his family before those white-power pricks turned them into fish bait."

"What happened?" I asked.

"I failed," Harry said. "It still haunts me. Whenever I see one of these assholes, I want to beat the shit out of them, so thank you for doing that."

"He was going to kill me otherwise," I said. Every time a cop like Varney gives me crap about how bounty hunters scrape the bottom of humanity's barrel, I think about how much blood the police have on their hands. I've never had an informant murdered.

"Seems like he and his buddies already got some work done," Harry said. "We found two people in the shower in there, bags over their heads. I'm betting related to the dead girl."

"This sucks," I said.

"Gun or no, I'm going to take you in," he said. "Do a formal interview. You're too close to too many dead bodies, you understand?"

I sighed. "Let me call my lawyer. And my wife." I thought of Janine back at the hotel, drilling into me about broken promises. I might have a chance of surviving this chaos, but my remarriage seemed on thin ice.

X

The interrogation box stank of bleach, which failed to erase the scents of piss and fear-sweat. Johnny sat with me on the prisoner's side of the battered steel table as Harry played host, asking if we wanted coffee. I nodded. Police-station brew always tasted like crap but I wanted its warmth in my cold gut. The adrenaline from my fight with the Aryan had worn off, leaving my bones feeling hollow and my muscles deflated. I daydreamed of a chorizo burrito and a cold beer.

Today Johnny looked like an attorney straight out of central casting. He wore a black suit cut to slim his thick torso, along with a black shirt and red tie. While we waited for Harry to return with the coffee, he pulled out his phone and swiped through messages, alternately nodding or shaking his head.

"Thank you for coming," I told him.

"It's my job," he said. "But sooner or later, we're going to be square, okay? I know you and your sister did a lot for me, but I got paying clients."

"Understood," I said, and left it at that. A police station seemed like the wrong place to bring up our history, and the dead body we shared.

The door opened, framing Harry with three paper cups

of coffee in his massive hands. He passed them out, and I took a sip of mine. It tasted like burnt earth, not unpleasant, instead of liquified cow manure. "Not bad," I said.

"We make it good because we got to drink it," Harry said, taking the seat across from us. "You think we want to drink crap?"

"It's not about what you want," I said. "Since it's our tax dollars at work, I figured your office manager would go cheap as possible."

Harry snorted. "Yeah, right. With your tax dollars, we got ourselves a badass coffeemaker. It got little pods, you know, with the individual flavors? I'm a big fan of this one called Morning Blend. That's what you're drinking."

"But it's night," Johnny offered.

"You're a genius of observation," Harry said. "Caffeine's good any time of day, am I right? Especially if that day's looking like it'll be long."

Johnny nudged his cup an inch away from him. "If you're not going to charge my client, why are we here? My client's more than happy to cooperate, but he has nothing to do…"

Harry let his head droop to his chest, as if Johnny had pushed a spine-cracking boulder onto his back. "Work with me, man. Our Nazi friend's coated in blood, his prints are all over the trailer. Meanwhile your client's here without a speck on him. He's not who I want, and we all know it. I just want a little information."

I sipped my coffee and waited.

"Let me appeal to your ego," Harry said to me, reaching into his jacket and pulling out his phone. "You tell me what happened in that trailer, maybe it gives me something to use on the suspect. He cracks, helps me roll up a bunch of

Aryans? You earn a big favor in my book, okay?"

I thought about that bloody kitchen, and the trailer's residents spending their final minutes in terror and pain. "Okay."

Johnny twitched. "Not okay."

I turned to him. "I'll speak slow. I begin a sentence you don't like, shush me."

Johnny groaned like a dying ox and nodded. Harry placed his phone on the table, flicked it to life, and double-tapped an icon of a microphone. "You mind if I record this?"

"No," I said.

Harry tapped a red circle on his screen. "Test," he said, and the red circle pulsed. A series of numbers appeared beneath, counting upward from zero. "Test, test."

"Cool app," I said.

"Yeah. Saves us money on recorders, which we can spend on coffee. Now tell me what went down."

I gave him almost everything, leaving out my meeting with Frankie. As I spoke, he probed the edges of my narrative, trying to tease out the loose threads, but thirty years of living with a felonious sibling had taught me how to keep my lies nice and tight.

When I finished, he sat back and said: "That was some fine bullshit."

"Not appropriate," Johnny said.

"I don't understand what you mean," I said.

"Oh, it makes sense, a lot of sense. Except for the giant-ass hole in the middle of it all. Someone just called you on the phone, told you where to go? I wouldn't buy that in a movie, man."

I smirked. "Like I told you back at the trailer park, people call me all the time. My number's everywhere. It's probably written on the bathroom walls of every bar between here and Salt Lake City."

Harry smiled. "Right next to your sister's, no doubt."

I returned the smile, not taking the bait. "Cheap shot, Detective."

"Had to say it. She's a thorn in our side, son."

"Oh, I know. I got pulled over the other day? One of your cops got in my face about her. It was harassment. He wouldn't even let me pick up my trash."

Harry's smile wavered. "What? Which officer?"

"Last name's Varney."

Harry's smile shriveled to a frown. "I know that guy. He's a clown. I know you don't think much of us, but we're not all like that. Stay clear, you see him again."

"We're getting off-topic here," Johnny said. "Can we please stick with the incident tonight? Otherwise we're walking out."

I lifted my coffee cup in mock salute. "Anyway, cops usually bring Frankie up in a couple seconds. You held out a whole twenty minutes after we sat down."

"I'm not stupid enough to ask you to give her up," Harry said. "My colleagues have tried that before. But I'll tell you to listen to your conscience. We know you meet with her. We know you're probably doing things for her. That big shootout at that quarry, when Zombie Bill got blown up like something out of a movie? We're sure she was there, and maybe you, too. Nobody else local has access to that sort of firepower."

I said nothing.

Harry shoved his chair back and stood, bracing his hands on the table as he leaned forward. "My point is, one day she's going to bring you down. And maybe you don't care, because blood counts for a lot. But you care about your wife and daughter. And you care about the life you've built. Think about that the next time she wants you to help kill a couple meth dealers."

"We better go," Johnny said quietly. "This interview is over."

"By the way," I said. "Can I get back my guns you took?"

"We haven't finished testing them."

"Which means you haven't started." I sighed. "So when do I get them back? Ten years from now? Twenty? Never?" Good thing I had locked my remaining pistol in the trunk of my car before entering the station, rather than checking it into the lockers behind the reception desk: this bastard might have found a way to finally seize that one, too.

Snorting Harry yanked open the door of the interrogation room. With a sarcastic bow, he waved us into the corridor beyond. Without so much as glancing at him, I took a left and headed for the front door, Johnny on my heels. After the chemical stink of the box, the musty hallway smelled beautiful.

"I'm on the verge," Johnny said, once we had passed out of Harry's earshot.

"The verge of what?"

"Telling you not to call me anymore," he said, his cheeks flushed. "You plunge right into these gray areas."

"I live in the gray areas," I corrected him.

"Okay," he said, raising his voice. "You want to go philosophical tough-guy on me? Okay. But the next time you want me to put up with this, you're paying for the privilege, you hear? And I don't think you can afford me. Good night."

"Good night," I said, and slowed my walk so he could slip past me and out the station's front doors. I lingered beneath the television in the waiting area, giving him a few minutes to drive away. He was a man of wild moods, that Johnny. Probably not the best thing for a lawyer, but I had my issues, too.

It seemed like a quiet night at the station. The cop at the front desk pecked away at a keyboard attached to an antique screen. On wooden benches before him, a small crowd waited for an officer or detective to arrive and tell them something. A few wore the shiny suits of ambulance-chasing lawyers, but the only thing in common among the rest was a shared look of trauma: vacant stares, clenched hands, bloodless faces. Their shared pain made me turn away, toward the television murmuring the latest tragedy: a candlelit vigil for Charles Beevoir, the football star gunned down at that convenience store. The biggest mass shooting since, well, the day my sister sent Zombie Bill and his men straight to hell.

The screen flashed a photo of the teenager, smiling wide for the camera.

My heart stopped.

The floor dropped out from under me.

Before I could say a word to the desk cop, a scream erupted from deep in the station. Not the roars of an angry perp dragged off to a holding cell, or a cop raging at some poor sap of a prisoner. Screams of pain. Dying, maybe.

The desk cop shoved his keyboard away and sprinted down the corridor toward that horrible noise, followed by a rush of police from the offices beyond the waiting area.

My smart move would have been to slip out, climb in my truck, and drive away. I had left a voicemail for Janine about meeting with the cops, so she was probably worried about me—and if she wasn't, I had bigger problems. Instead I pushed through the swinging door in the waist-high barrier that separated the waiting area from the rest of the station, following the chaos. Something told me I needed to see what was happening.

I made it to the end of the corridor before a cop clamped my shoulder hard enough to stop me cold. He began dragging me away, roaring about trespassing, but not before I saw the bloodshed through the paint-chipped bars of the holding cells.

My Viking friend was face-down on the concrete, at the center of a spreading pool of blood. The back of his orange coveralls riddled with red marks. Someone had shanked him. The cops formed a line between the body and a mass of screaming prisoners, and I heard the dull thwack of a baton smacking flesh.

Harry straddled the Viking and jammed two fingers into the blood-slick neck, shaking his head even as he screamed for a medic.

I let the cop push me down the corridor and into the waiting area, where the civilians milled like anxious cattle. I wondered if one of them knew the dead man, and for the briefest of instants I felt sorry, if not for my attacker, then for the relative or friend left in fear. Then I ran into the night, looking over my shoulder for pursuit.

XI

A few miles from my hotel, I pulled onto the side of the road and placed my forehead against the steering wheel and took deep breaths until the nausea retreated.

I was thinking about Iraq, and waking up some mornings with insects crawling into my open mouth, or down my ass-crack.

The stink of chemical smoke from the villages burning along the canals.

A bystander at a Baghdad intersection lifting a phone to his ear, and the street exploding in dust and rock.

A woman in a black hijab holding out pieces of her dead boy as if I could somehow put him back together.

And how, on night raids, when we stacked beside the door of a target house, we would hear the jihadists inside chanting as they prepared to die.

When I returned to Idaho after my discharge, I had hoped that the worst of my life was behind me. And for many years, that seemed to be the case. Thanks to therapy, I panicked less whenever I saw a bearded man answer a phone on the street. I quit drinking so much. I had to practice my breathing exercises whenever I heard fireworks, but I chose to believe that my trauma would scar over, given enough time.

I was wrong about all of that. Maybe people like me are incapable of living normal lives, no matter how badly we want one.

Although it took a little longer, I stuck to side streets on the way back to the hotel, circling blocks and retracing routes in case someone was following me. In our room, I found Janine lying on the bed, watching a sitcom on her laptop. When she saw my face, she slapped the screen closed and slid toward me.

"What happened?" she asked.

Instead of embracing her, I marched over to the sideboard and poured myself a whiskey, choosing to ignore her frown. "Charles Beevoir," I said.

"Who?"

"The kid at the gas station. The one who got shot, remember?"

"Yeah?"

"He was the boyfriend of the dead girl in our safe," I said.

She sighed and let her head sag forward. "Oh, babe, this is bad."

"I found the girl's address," I continued. "Frankie found it for me. I drove over there, and saw a photo of him on her fridge. I have zero doubt. His face is all over the news."

"So that's why you met with the cops?"

I nodded and sipped my drink, prepping myself for the next twist in the conversation. "I got attacked by someone at the girl's place," I said, as calmly as possible. "But it's okay, he's dead."

"Dead?"

Screw it: I downed the whiskey. The alcohol hit my

stomach like napalm, making me wince. "Someone shanked him in jail. I saw the body, it's okay."

Her voice quavered. "How is that remotely okay? What's going on?"

"Working on that, dear." I uncorked the bottle and poured myself another few fingers of high-proof goodness. This drink burned harder as it made its way to my stomach. The world fuzzed pleasantly at the edges.

"Any connection with your work?" she asked.

I slammed the cup down hard enough to make her jump. "Believe me when I tell you, babe, that I did nothing to bring this to our doorstep, okay?"

Janine set the laptop aside and stood. "Do not use that tone with me."

I stared down the neck of the whiskey bottle, which from this angle bore more than a passing resemblance to a gun barrel. Jamming the cork home, I opened a bag of potato chips and shoveled a handful into my mouth. Anything not to talk.

Janine sighed. "Look. We're not in a good place."

My mouth full of crunch and salt, I nodded.

"Part of it is this hotel room. I feel like I'm in a trap." She struggled against the smile tugging the edges of her lips. "A very, very hip trap."

I swallowed my chips and cleared my throat. "Maybe we can grab the kid, drive up into the hills," I said. "Someplace with Wi-Fi, so you can work. We hang out until this all blows over. The cops are on it. Frankie's on it."

"No," she said. "Cops don't care about us. Frankie is Frankie, no offense. We need to handle it. And I'm going to help however I can, because if I just sit here, I'll lose my mind. I'll tap things until my fingers bleed. You know it kills stress to actually get out there and do something, as opposed to just being…a…a lump."

The idea of Janine within ten miles of a gunfight or an axe-swinging lunatic made my stomach drop like an elevator with a cut cable. Before I could open my mouth and deep-six that idea, though, my phone buzzed in my jeans pocket. "Speak of the devil," I said, and swiped the device to life.

"Heard you had a spot of trouble," Frankie said, trying on a corny British accent.

"What did you hear?"

"That you were present when the cops kicked a member of the Brotherhood's ass. That the dude got stabbed in holding. A lot of very bad people are upset right now."

Giving Janine a just-one-minute gesture, I left the room and shut the door behind me. "Upset at who?" I scanned the balcony for any eavesdroppers. The restaurant below was empty, along with the intersection in front of the hotel.

She sighed. "Not at you, in case you're wondering. You're getting me an awesome Christmas gift this year, because I've spent the past hour on the phone telling people that you had nothing to do with anything. Wrong place, wrong time."

I knew that Frankie sold weapons to anyone with the cash. That meant members of the Aryan Brotherhood, white supremacist militias, and any other scumbag group. She also sold weapons to people who shot white supremacists by the truckload. If nothing else, Frankie believed in the principle of free markets. "They trust you on that?" I asked.

"For now," she said. "You weren't anywhere near the dude when he got shanked, so most parties are apparently cool with it. As far as they know, it was the cops who beat the dude down before he ended up in holding. That true?"

"No, it was me." For once, I was glad that the cops took the credit for a collar. "He came at me with an axe. I had to put him down."

She sighed again. "This is heavy."

"What was a neo-Nazi scumbag doing in that trailer, anyway?" I struggled to keep my volume down. "That dead girl in my house, her boyfriend was that dude who got shot at that gas station near our place. I have no idea what's going on, but whatever it is, it's really weird. And maybe big."

"Well, here's the good news: this isn't an Aryan beef. They're just hired guns, doing cleanup."

"So what's the bad news?"

"Um, that someone's paying the Aryans to do cleanup. Which means whoever's behind all this, they're a pretty heavy hitter, wouldn't you say?"

"I was just telling Janine, maybe we should get out of town, take refuge somewhere."

"You know that won't help. We need to get aggressive." Across the street from the hotel, a pair of headlights flashed. "You see me?"

"If you're the one in the black SUV," I said.

"I am indeed," she replied. "Grab Janine and come on. I don't want to get too dramatic, because I know that makes you totally freak out, but we're going to do some detective work, then we're probably going to war."

"I won't put my wife in harm's way," I said.

"First, she's not made of friggin' spun sugar. Second, she's way smarter than you, and I'll need her brainpower. Third, you can't keep her cooped up in a hotel room. You said it yourself, it might not be safe anymore."

In Iraq, things had seemed so simple: kill or be killed. Survive to see another day. Try to stay hydrated in hundred-degree heat while wearing full body armor and toting a rifle. Now home sweet home had turned just as deadly. Whatever I did to deserve this, Lord, I'm sorry.

XII

"What did I just tell you a minute ago? I'm going crazy, staying here," Janine said. "We'll be safer with Frankie, anyway. She's got all those men with guns, right?"

"If something happened to you…"

"Something might happen to me right here. You can't guarantee anything." She stuck out a fist. "I'll rock-paper-scissors you for it."

"What?"

"Come on," she said. "Best two out of three. If I win, I'm coming along. If I lose, I'll stay here."

I smiled despite myself. "You know I'm no good at this."

"That's because I have those ninja mind skills." She shook her fist. Her eyes bright, manic. "I know what you'll do before you do it. Come on."

"Maybe you go to Montana."

"And deal with your mom? I'd rather risk a bullet."

"This is serious."

She dropped her fist. "I know. I'm just trying to keep the fear back." Crossing her arms over her chest, she tapped her elbows five times. "It's all bad choices. But out of all those bad choices, I think the least bad is going with your sister, considering how much firepower she's got."

The point about guns was a good one. I had spent the

past few days thinking that if one more horrible thing happened this week—killing a bunch of people in the woods and setting the bodies on fire seemed like the next logical step—Janine would walk out on our remarriage. That thought terrified me, but not as much as the image of her dead in the dirt.

"Okay," I said. "You need to promise me one thing, though."

She slipped her wallet and phone in her jeans. "What's that?"

"If Frankie and I go down, you run, got it? You get clear. Don't look back. Don't argue with me on that."

Janine paused in mid-step. I saw the fear move through her, collapsing her shoulders an inch, widening her eyes a fraction. It was the kind of fear that made you sick and weak, and I knew that because I felt it, too.

"Okay," she said, making fists when she wanted to touch doorknobs or elbows a hundred times, a thousand. "Okay."

"And don't snark with Frankie, please?" I asked as I opened the door and ushered her through.

"I guarantee nothing," she called over her shoulder as we trotted down the stairwell to the ground level.

The left rear door of the waiting SUV swung open as we approached. Ducking my head inside, I discovered Frankie in the front passenger seat. She winked. Behind the wheel sat Barnes, her lieutenant, a huge lump of muscle in a good suit.

"Where's the Monkey Man?" I asked as we climbed inside.

"Trust me, it's better if you don't know," Frankie said. "It involves something bad at a drive-in. By the way, took you long enough in there."

"We were fighting," Janine said cheerfully, as she pushed me into the back seat. "He didn't want me to come because he's afraid I'm delicate. He forgets I gave birth to our daughter, and that was way more pain than he'd ever be able to handle."

"Sounds like his usual macho bullshit," Frankie said. "I told him you were better off with us."

"We're all here, okay?" I said. "Can we get on with it?"

"If you insist." Frankie nodded to Barnes. "Drive, big guy."

If you asked a mad scientist to create, through the wonders of genetic engineering, a human being capable of taking all manner of blunt trauma without much damage to his or her major organs, whatever came out of the vat would look a lot like Barnes. For starters, he lacked a neck. His head was a bone wrecking-ball perched atop shoulders as hard and angled as castle battlements. His torso was a cylinder of muscle and bone, and his arms, straining against the fabric of his well-tailored suit, looked big enough to rip the head off an elephant without much effort. Frankie paid him well, and with good reason: he was worth five of her regular guys.

"Lovely to see you, Janine," Barnes said, always the gentleman, as he shifted the SUV into drive and pulled away from the curb. "Hey, Jake."

"Hey," I said, before leaning forward to slap my sister on the shoulder, hard. "That's for that 'macho bullshit' quip."

Frankie offered me a middle finger. Two left turns set us on a path to the highway onramp. Frankie pulled out her phone, tapped open the map app, and fiddled with little dots on the landscape. "Dude shot dead in a convenience store," she said. "Next night, his girlfriend's dead body in your house."

"Yeah," I said.

"You know Louie the mortician?"

"Of course. I think he's planted everyone in our family over the years."

"I use him sometimes as a source, in case I have a real vexing question about death. Sweet dude once you get to know him. He's also gay, you know that?"

"He ever date his customers?"

Frankie snorted. "Anyway, Louie likes to be paid in drink. So this afternoon, I take him out, thinking he might give me some info on the dead girl in your safe. We're downing shots until you can smell alcohol coming out of his pores. He reaches into his jacket pocket and pulls out this giant plastic screw. And he says, 'You know what that is?'

"I say, 'A screw?'

"He says, 'No, dummy, it's a butt plug.'

"He starts laughing and says: 'We just put this up the butts of corpses, so they don't leak all their fluids out their rear exit, if you know what I mean. And it's been my great pleasure to ram this massive piece of hardened plastic up the anal cavity of every dead anti-gay bigot in this county for the past twenty years. They spend eternity getting pegged.'"

"We got to all find our happiness where we can," I said.

"Then Louie asked why I was buying him drinks. I asked about the dead girl. Turns out, her body hasn't been released yet. But he did start talking about that kid at the gas station. He had seen that corpse, and it really freaked him out."

"Why?" Janine asked.

"Cluster of shots on the sternum, so tight you could put

a quarter over it, in his words." Frankie tapped her chest three times. "That's military shooting, and although people in our fair state buy a large number of guns—trust me on that one—you don't see that kind of precision very often. Louie didn't like the idea of some former soldier robbing convenience stores, shooting the customers. He said our veterans shouldn't be in that position."

"I got a question," Janine asked.

"I might have an answer," Frankie said.

"Why is Louie walking around with a butt plug for corpses?"

Frankie laughed. "I don't think we want to know. Back to the topic at hand: I didn't know that our various bodies were connected, but now that I do, it's just adding to the layers of worry here."

"So we got a military or ex-military shooter popping a kid along with a couple of other folks in a gas station," I said. "The next night, the kid's girlfriend ends up in my safe with a small-caliber bullet in her."

"And she was naked," Janine said. "If that has anything to do with anything."

"You're right," Frankie said. "Probably not the same killer for both. And among my contacts, there's been a disturbing lack of chatter about either of these murders. Usually when someone gets whacked in a weird way, there's a whole lot of buzz about why it happened, who did who wrong, blah-blah. But in this case? Radio silence. Which makes me interested."

"Why?" Janine asked.

"Besides the fact it's put my beloved brother in a spot of trouble, radio silence means something big and unusual is going on," Frankie said. "Big and unusual usually ends up being a threat to my little business, one way or another."

I nodded out the window. "So where are we going?"

"The boyfriend's house," Frankie said. "He lived in Meridian."

We went quiet. Barnes took the opportunity to turn the radio to a heavy metal station, his massive head bouncing to the beat, his shoulders shifting side to side with the guitar solos. It was like watching a landslide. Based on how Janine clutched my hand, she seemed afraid all that slipping and sliding would tip the SUV over, but the car roared its merry way into the sprawl.

When I was a kid, the area around Meridian was mostly fields dotted with farmhouses. Over the decades, suburban subdivisions had sprung up, with cookie-cutter houses arranged on neat lawns. Things had stayed that way until a few years ago, when those rich Californians began settling in southern Idaho, buying up land to build their drywall monstrosities. The strip-mall at one of the largest intersections had grown like a tumor into a massive structure of faux-Italian architecture, complete with a twelve-screen multiplex and a chain restaurant where you could eat an infinite amount of overcooked pasta for twelve bucks.

"It's so ugly," I said as we passed it. "Remember when there was that great view of the hills?"

"Yeah, but that was a long time ago," Frankie said. "And some developers wanted to make a lot of money."

A quick turn down a side street put those garish lights behind us. "Police already went over the kid's place, I'm assuming," I said. "And I bet our neo-Nazi friends paid a visit, too. You ask if he had connections to White Power?"

Frankie shook her head. "He didn't. And neither did his girlfriend."

"His parents' home?"

"His parents are dead," Frankie said. "Overdosed last year, within a month of each other. Usual story. He was already eighteen, so he could live alone without adult supervision."

"Here we are," Barnes said, sliding the SUV to the curb and killing the lights. Across the street stood a one-story ranch house with an attached garage. I knew Charles Beevoir had lived there because of the yellow police tape strung over the door. Unlike its neighbors, the house looked ill kept, the lawn a jungle of tall weeds and prickly bushes, the driveway littered with hoses and rusting engine parts.

We climbed out, Barnes unbuttoning his suit coat as he strode the overgrown walkway to the front door. Frankie followed, drawing a stubby pistol from beneath her jacket and pressing it against her leg. I kept my weapon holstered. I figured we had enough firepower already.

Barnes knocked on the door and tried the knob. Locked. Nodding to Janine, he stepped off the stoop and disappeared into the darkness around the side of the house. He might have been solid as a brick shithouse, but he moved with the grace of a panther. I heard the faint pop of breaking glass, the hiss of a window sliding open.

The door opened, and Barnes ushered us inside. We entered a disaster of a living room, so filthy it was hard to tell where the kid's mess ended and the cops' ransacking began. A narrow path cut through the piles of clothes, books, and pizza boxes to the rear of the house. The stink of mold and old food forced me to breathe through my mouth. I glanced at Janine, who wrinkled her nose and clenched her hands into a ball against her chest.

"This is what happens," Frankie whispered, "when you

let a teenager live by himself."

I assumed a football star would have taken a bit more pride in his surroundings. Then again, losing his parents might have shoved his mind into a deep hole. "Hush," I said.

The bedroom was less of an OCD sufferer's nightmare, with the exception of the disheveled bed. Shelves of trophies and ripped posters of football stars lined the walls. The sportsman had been a bit of a geek, too. Beside the closet, a stack of plastic bins bristled with stripped-down equipment: lenses, speakers, circuit boards, tangles of wires, thickets of screws and nails. A toolkit in the top bin held wire strippers, wrenches, screwdrivers, and a multimeter.

"Someone took his computer," Frankie said, pointing at an empty space on the desk, where a laptop power cord curled like a lonely snake. Next to the desk, on a small coated-wire shelf, sat a hollow plastic cube, open at the sides, with a metal plate at its base.

"What's that?" Janine asked. She stood in the cleanest part of the room, an open area between the bed and the closet, with her hands still fisted tight.

"A 3D printer," I said. "They're pretty useless, unless you want to make a Yoda figure in glow-in-the-dark plastic, or something."

Frankie sorted through the hardware in the bins until she found an old smartphone. "Surprised they didn't take this," she said, before flipping it over. "Oh, never mind." The screen was a web of cracks.

"Still useful," Barnes said.

"True," Frankie said. "Hopefully the insides aren't smashed to shit. Grab the printer and let's get out of here."

Barnes unplugged the 3D printer from the wall, slipped

it under his arm, and headed for the door, Janine tight on his heels. Pocketing the phone, Frankie followed them. I took a last journey around the room, using a pencil to poke through the papers and small bits of hardware on the desk. Until tonight, the kid had been nothing to me but a face on the news. Now he was a person, an interesting mix of brainy and sporty—and he was gone forever. This room was a shell. Paranoid of fingerprints, I wiped the pencil clean with the edge of my shirt and tossed it in the trash.

Back in the SUV, Frankie examined the dead boy's phone, rubbing her finger over the fingerprint reader, and nodded, satisfied. "It's an Android," she said. "That's good." Rooting through the shoulder bag at her feet, she retrieved a universal charger and plugged the phone into a dashboard port. After the device had charged for a few seconds, she turned it on. From the back seat I sensed her holding her breath.

The screen flickered to life, the Android logo reduced to green shards by the shattered glass. The password screen popped into view. Frankie exhaled and set the phone on the dashboard, letting the battery fill.

"What's the plan?" I asked.

"Back to my ranch," she said. "We got some work to do."

"What was the point of this?" Janine asked, her tone sharp. Her hand tapped the door handle a dozen times, two dozen, before shifting to touch either end of the armrest, back and forth, back and forth. I reached for her knee, and she knocked my hand away. I took no offense, although I felt a little guilty for not escorting her out of the house when we first saw it was a hoarder's nest.

Barnes cocked an eyebrow, unused to people speaking

to Frankie like that.

"Finding the boy's trail," Frankie said evenly. "Let's go."

Following the loss of her beloved shipping container, Frankie drifted between three houses on a random schedule. We took the highway back to Boise, exiting near Table Rock, a rich neighborhood with commanding views of the valley. I knew Frankie's house here, a two-story stucco block well shaded by ancient pines, with a small round pool in the back and a two-bay garage. It was tiny compared to the sprawling homes on either side, but what it lacked in square footage, it made up in defenses.

The front door, wood on the outside, was plated with steel on the inside. The first floor was monastery-level empty, its blankness interrupted only by a few pieces of antique furniture and a scarred wooden dining table. Heavy black blinds covered every window. If I knew my sister, the white walls covered an army of guns, stored on pegs between the studs. I wouldn't have been surprised if she had installed a few claymore mines around the property to discourage intruders.

After setting the 3D printer on the dining table, Barnes fetched four plastic bottles of water from the fridge in the kitchen. While we rehydrated, Frankie knelt and worked her fingers into a crack between the floorboards, which hinged back to reveal a small safe in the subflooring. An eight-digit combination popped the safe open, revealing a laptop.

"My safe is bigger than yours," I said.

"Hasn't Janine told you that size doesn't matter?" Frankie said, plugging the laptop into the port on the backside of the 3D printer. She tapped a few keys, awakening a browser and a few programs I didn't recognize.

"What are we doing?" Janine asked.

The blocky typeface of a state government website flicked into view. "Here we go," Frankie said, tapping a passcode. The initial screen disappeared, replaced by a mugshot of Charles Beevoir. "He had a pot bust. They dropped the charges, but I'm surprised they kept him on the football team. He must have been a hell of a player."

"You know, I got access to those databases," I said. "You could have just asked me to log in for you."

"I'm using your password," Frankie said. "Next time, think up something that's not your wife's birthday, okay?"

My cheeks reddening, I sipped my water and stared at the screen. Frankie scrolled down to the kid's fingerprint section, the whorls and swirls of ten digits in separate boxes, and clicked to download each to her desktop. Then she opened a new program and dragged the ten images into a blank field.

The 3D printer snapped to life, humming as it poured strips of hot plastic onto the metal plate. We sat and sipped our water and watched as it slowly built a small yellow tower that, after a few minutes, assumed a familiar shape.

"Are you printing a finger?" I asked.

"We're printing ten fingers," Frankie said. "The kid's fingerprints, to be exact, from his file."

"Will plastic fingerprints work on a phone?" Janine asked.

Frankie smirked. "And therein lies the rub. I've done this before, and it works maybe half the time. Older phones are more forgiving than the newer ones. I don't know if it's because of the sensors or what."

"Older Android," Barnes said from the kitchen.

"Newer software, if the phone's been dormant a couple

of days, it also asks for a password in addition to the fingerprint," Frankie continued. "Hopefully this kid didn't update this phone before he tossed it in the bin."

"Where'd you learn about all this?" I asked.

"Read about some criminals in Brazil doing it, so I asked around. Turns out the cops have been doing it for a couple years, in limited cases, to unlock suspects' phones. Only they keep their technique a secret. I suspect they're using something a little more advanced than I am."

The printer crapped out its hot plastic millimeter by painful millimeter. Say what you will about the future, it's a little rough and slow around the edges. While we waited, Frankie removed a crumpled pack of cigarettes from her pocket, along with a box of wooden matches. Coffin nail between her lips, ready to torch up, she noticed Janine looking at her.

"What?" Frankie said.

Janine frowned.

"I tried giving up for a couple weeks," Frankie said. "Seriously, I did. But it's going to be a long night, and I need the nicotine."

Without a word, Janine picked up her chair and carried it to the far side of the room before sitting down again. I stayed in place, acting as a DMZ between the two women, who continued to glance at each other as Frankie breathed smoke.

"Want to hear a joke?" Barnes called from the kitchen.

"Not now," Frankie said, making sure Janine saw she was taking her time with the cigarette. By the time she finished, the printer's first two digits had printed and cooled. Stubbing out her smoke against her chair leg, Frankie slipped the thin plastic sheaths over her right thumb and forefinger, picked up the phone, and pressed the finger-print sensor. The thumb worked. The lock screen gave way to the apps menu.

"So this is his old phone, right?" Janine said. "Where's his current one?"

"Cops never found it," Frankie said, tapping the apps. "That's what one of my contacts in the department told me. Hopefully he didn't wipe this one before he got a new device."

"Use that app that lets you find your phone," I said. "It's right on the home screen. It might show us where his current device is."

"You're not as dumb as you look," Frankie said, tapping the appropriate logo. Frowning, she angled the screen so I could see a map. A red pin stabbed the middle of a bright green mass. Flicking her fingers, she zoomed out until I saw the blue curve of the Snake River, and a scattering of town names I recognized. It was maybe ten miles north of my house.

"Go a little right," I said. A warm hand on my back, Janine peering over my shoulder at the screen. I pointed out the faint gridwork of Parma. "There's the convenience store where everybody got shot. Also not that far."

"What are you thinking?" Janine asked.

"Something happened in this area with the dot, something that forced them to run," I said. "Whatever it was, it was bad enough to make him drop his phone there and not pick it up again."

"We should head out there," Frankie said.

I glanced at Janine. "You okay with this?"

Janine nodded and squeezed my shoulder, hard.

Frankie raised her head. "Barnes, you want to call in

some extra help?"

Standing in the doorway, Barnes nodded and reached into his suit jacket for his phone. As he tapped out a text message, Frankie looked at me. "You want to load up? We got some pieces in the safe upstairs. The big one. The one that's bigger than yours."

I remembered that day in the quarry, Janine bragging about her armory as Zombie Bill burned. "Sure," I said. "And if we could stop the size jokes, that'd be great."

"What's wrong? Feeling unmanned?"

"Um, you're my sister." I wrinkled my nose.

"If you two are going to argue all night," Janine said, "maybe I need a gun, too."

XIII

Frankie's safe held ten rifles. I helped myself to a semi-automatic short-barreled carbine with a folding stock, and three magazines of 5.56 ammunition. Janine chose a 9mm of the same make and model she had used on the range at home. Between those weapons and my own pistol, I thought we had enough firepower to take on anything waiting for us in the night.

I hoped so, at least.

Frankie's safe made me think of my own safe at home, and Ruth Jenner's silver necklace tucked away in its drawer. That poor girl. By now, she was either a pile of ash or headed underground, and once her next of kin cleared her stuff out of the bloody trailer, that little piece of jewelry would be the only sign she ever existed.

"I'm sorry," I said.

"What?" Janine asked.

"Nothing."

I stepped outside the house in time to see Frankie finish a call. "Backup's arriving in a few minutes," she said, slipping her phone into her pocket.

"And we're bringing Barnes, right?" I asked, nodding to the man-mountain standing on the far side of the SUV. "He's a walking platoon."

His stony expression never shifting, Barnes offered me a thumbs-up.

"Safety in numbers, dude," Frankie said. "But you need to make me a promise."

"What's that?"

"If things get rough, you need to let me do what I do best, okay? No matter how rough it gets, I don't want you whining or whatever."

I lifted my rifle. "Hello? Army? A couple of tours?" On the surface, I was all bravado. On the inside, I was a bag of frayed nerves. I regretted not checking Frankie's fridge for a beer before leaving the house. The alcohol might have calmed my nerves. I remembered shitting my pants from fear during my first firefight in Baghdad, and continuing to shoot and duck and sprint as cooling diarrhea ran down my leg. One of my proudest moments, come to think of it. Whatever else happened tonight, I wanted to avoid that sort of mess.

"Sorry," Frankie said. "You've been in the shit."

You have no idea, I thought. "So cool it."

She clapped her hands on my shoulders and angled her head to mine, her face stiff with mock seriousness. "Sorry, bro."

A few minutes later, another SUV appeared on the road below the house, flashing its lights as it stopped beside the mailbox. In the front seats I saw two of Frankie's people, tattooed, pierced, and ready for war. She recruited lean boys from the rougher bars around here.

We climbed into Frankie's SUV, Barnes at the wheel, and left Boise. The city peeled away, then the suburban sprawl, and soon enough we cruised through a darkness broken only by the yellow glow from grain silos and fenced-in truckyards. I set the rifle barrel-down between my knees and focused on my breathing—deep in, pause, deep out. I wondered whether Barnes and the SUV behind us should double back, change routes, anything to avoid a tail.

"Janine," I said. "Round check."

Janine drew her pistol and checked for a round in the chamber with a speed and precision that made me proud. In the dimness I saw her eyes gleaming—maybe fear, but a little excitement, too.

"Can I ask something intensely personal?" Frankie asked.

"Sure," Janine said, holstering her weapon. "But you might not get an answer."

Frankie snorted. "What made you two decide to get back together?"

"We decided to work through it," Janine said. "For the kid. And also because we put so much time in. It was a lot to throw away."

I placed my hand in hers.

We cruised another fifteen minutes down the two-lane paralleling the Snake River, the water glinting silver under the rising moon. Few people lived in this stretch. I only saw a light or two. Frankie, consulting her phone, reaching over and tapped Barnes on the shoulder.

Barnes spun the wheel, our headlights illuminating a dirt trail that cut away from the main road and toward the river. I glanced at the second SUV turning after us, right as its driver clicked off the headlights. It became a blob of deeper black, lost as soon as I looked away.

"Here," Frankie said, tapping Barnes on the shoulder again. Slotting the phone into her jacket, she drew the pistol from her hip holster and racked the slide. Twisting around in her seat to face us, she said: "I'm just selling what the kids want."

It was a joke from our teenage years, when Frankie sold chopped-up herbs to middle schoolers.

"And the kids want humiliation," I said, completing the old phrase, before opening my door and stepping out into the insect-humming night. In her seat, Janine raised the pistol, asking silently if she should bring it with her. I shook my head: even if we weren't the only people for twenty miles around, we already had enough between my rifle and whatever Frankie and Barnes carried. Janine placed the weapon on the floor of the SUV and scooted out the open door.

Barnes appeared beside the hood, buttoning his coat against the wind.

Pausing once to check her phone, Frankie trotted into the field, never looking back. I followed her flickering shadow, holding the rifle at port arms, Janine on my heels. At the furthest penumbra of the headlights, where the glow shaded to yellow before the darkness ate it whole, a strand of barbed wire glimmered between a pair of wooden posts. Frankie knelt and folded back the tall grass until her hand hit something dark and shiny.

Barking laughter, she held up a phone, its case shattered. Awoken by the motion, the screen popped to life: an oversized battery icon flashing red. "God bless modern technology," she said.

"I guess," I said. "But that doesn't tell us what they were doing out here."

We heard two deep thumps from the darkness behind us. Frankie hit the grass at a healthy fraction of light-speed. My body, acting on instinct before my brain fully processed the sound, turned and hurled itself at a confused

Janine, who squawked as I slammed her into the dirt.

Standing in front of the lit headlights of the SUV, Barnes paused for a half-second too long. His shoulder spat red, and he winced. Another thump. He dipped his knees, and a black line opened along the side of his close-cropped head. The driver's side mirror popped in a bright burst of glass and metal.

Frankie rose to one knee and popped off a shot in the direction of the thumps. Janine beneath me moaned in fear.

In front of the SUV, Barnes reached into his jacket and drew his pistol. Dropping to a knee, he edged around the side of the hood and pulled the trigger four times, illuminating the field like lightning strikes. In those brief flashes I saw the second SUV skewed thirty yards behind ours, its windshield shattered in two places, and a black figure ducking behind its rear bumper.

"Covering," Frankie said, and fired her pistol again.

"Moving," I said, and pointed for Janine to crawl behind Frankie. She did, and I followed. No cover out here, just tall grass. I felt forty feet tall and a hundred feet wide, a bullet magnet in the SUV's headlights. The darkness was our friend.

Once Janine and I made it a few yards beyond Frankie, I stood and slotted my rifle against my shoulder and yelled: "Covering."

Frankie took the cue to rise and retreat behind me as I fired half the magazine at the second SUV and the shooter. Passing close, she flattened her hand and made a swooping motion: let's flank this fucker. I nodded.

Another thump, and lead zipped overhead.

Popping over the hood of our SUV, Barnes fired again. His right side shiny with blood. He squeezed off another two rounds before the top of his head exploded in a pink mist. Man-mountain or no, he went down hard.

Sighting on the burst that downed Barnes, Frankie fired once. Out in the dark, someone screamed, high and loud as a rabbit in a snare. I fired and moved again, Janine's breath loud beside me. I dared to hope that Frankie had nailed the shooter.

That was before three new muzzle flashes bloomed near the road. Rounds whistled and snapped past us. The ground near my foot burst, spraying my face with dirt and bits of grass.

With the magazines in my pants and whatever Frankie had on her, we had enough ammunition to bang it out with our attackers for another few minutes, then we would end up like Barnes. If we made it to the river, Frankie and Janine would have a chance to escape in the water while I held my ground. I would fight until I ran out of ammo, then I would use the rifle as a club, then I would sink my teeth into my enemies' necks if it came to that.

A loud boom cut off the wounded man in mid-shriek. Another burst to our left, close behind our SUV, and Frankie cursed as the rounds zipped past her head. Whoever these guys were, they must have forgotten to bring their night-vision goggles—why else would they keep missing us? I emptied the rest of my magazine in the direction of the most recent shooter and began reaching for a new one when Frankie whistled and pointed behind us.

Time to run.

Taking Janine's hand in mine, we joined my sister in sprinting as hard as we could for the river. The grass rose waist-high, crunchy and loud beneath our boots. In another few yards, we entered a patch of small trees, our attackers' rounds rattling the branches overhead. My lungs burned, and my bum left knee twinged dangerously as we vaulted over a log, but I thought we might make it. As we cleared that grove, and the river gleamed into view before us, the shots stopped.

That was odd.

The world went white, blinding. Headlights in front of us: three or four trucks, engines roaring to life. A dog barking frantic and loud. Janine screamed. Frankie in silhouette raised her pistol and fired. Glass shattered, and someone yelled. I raised the rifle and pulled the trigger, clicking on an empty chamber. With all the adrenaline sizzling my brain, I had forgotten to reload. Dumb rookie error.

Automatic fire mowed the grass in front of us. We stopped in our tracks, arms raised, panting. Every little muscle in Janine's face trembling, Frankie beside her with a clenched jaw and a murderous gaze.

"Let's stop with the running shit," called a deep voice from the light. "We got things to discuss."

Lord be praised, my underwear had remained poop-free.

PART 3
MY OWN PRIVATE IDAHO

I

With a bag that stank of mildew over my head, and my hands cuffed behind my back, my options had narrowed to controlling my breathing and trying to hear as much as possible. Tires hummed on a highway. Someone coughed to my left. Brakes squealed as we slowed for an exit.

You can figure out how to save them, I thought. You can buy yourself time. There's always a chance. Right until the end, there's always a chance.

My heartbeat slowed. I reviewed those final moments in the field, when rough hands snatched away my rifle and ammo. Squinting against the blinding headlights, I caught a glimpse of masked men in combat gear muscling Janine and Frankie into separate vehicles. No tattoos, no badges, no dog tags, no identifying marks on any of them. My rage was a live thing, ready to kill, and I thrashed against those hands holding my arms until my head exploded with pain and the lights went out.

My daughter was in Montana. Whatever happened here, she would live.

Wouldn't she?

A heavy operation like this would have no problem executing a kid. I had seen it dozens of times in Iraq. There is a breed of hard men who can pull the trigger on anyone if the mission demands it.

Against the blackness of the hood, I saw scenes from Baghdad. Kicking in doors of empty warehouses to find setups for jihad TV: cloth backdrops dark with Arabic script, crumpled tarps spattered with blood, camera tripods and bright lights positioned to capture every drop of righteous gore. Having your head sawed off on YouTube is a horrible way to die.

Stop drifting off, I thought. Keep your head clear.

The truck stopped. I heard the muffled squeal of brakes as other vehicles halted around us. Strong hands grabbed my shoulders and pulled me through an open door. Whispered conversation and the click of metal. I smelled a menthol cigarette. My feet touched gravel, and someone shoved me forward so hard I almost lost my balance.

The cool night air transitioned to a warmer space. A door slammed, and our boots echoed off wood and concrete. The hands pushed me into a hard, uncomfortable chair.

Before I took another breath, my hood whipped away. I blinked rapidly, trying to absorb as many details as possible—dark-oak walls lined with mounted deer and elk heads; a marble fireplace, the mantel heavy with framed daguerreotypes of settlers in wide hats and frocks; and in one corner, an enormous stuffed bear, paws raised in attack. A fat corgi trundled past, sniffing the floorboards as it disappeared through an open doorway to my left.

Not exactly the torture chamber I was expecting.

I tried turning my head to better see the man behind me. "Where am I?" I asked.

"Silence," he said. It was a voice I recognized but couldn't quite place.

Into the doorway stepped a middle-aged man: gray hair shaped by an expensive cut, sharp cheekbones, and the sort of gaze that coolly evaluates your worth. His leathery complexion suggested years spent under harsh sunlight. His smile revealed shiny, expensive teeth. He wore a well-tailored sport jacket over a black dress shirt and designer jeans. His crocodile boots probably cost more than my truck.

"Do you recognize me?" the man asked, cocking his head to study me.

"No," I said, truthfully.

"My name's Baker." He sounded like a radio announcer, smooth and musical. The voice that told you another hundred people had died in Syria, or that the President had decided to launch a nuke.

Whether or not Baker was his real name, that I could see his face was a bad sign. They never let you see their face if they plan on letting you live.

"Where are my people?" I asked.

Baker straightened his spine. "Concern for others. I like that. Usually they start off by asking what they're doing here."

"I figure I'll find that out anyway," I said.

Baker nodded. "True. Your sister and wife are safe. You'll see them shortly."

"Okay." I resisted the urge to spit on the polished floor, just to show my contempt. "So why am I here, Baker?"

"For the chance to make up for some old wrongs. You like the sound of that? Do right, and you'll come out of this just fine."

This guy produced more bullshit than a cattle farm. "Sure," I said. "Who doesn't like clearing the ledger?"

"Then let's get some food, and I'll walk you through the whole thing." He nodded to the man standing behind me. "Please unlock his cuffs."

I felt a cold hand on my wrists, a tug as the key slotted into the handcuffs, and a pop as the metal bands snapped open. I stood and turned around.

My old friend Varney stared back at me. He had traded in his cop uniform for black nylon pants and a long-sleeved shirt under a bullet-resistant vest, with a big silver pistol on his right hip. The costume made him look like a jihadi filming a beheading video. I fought the urge to tell him that as I rubbed the circulation back into my forearms. His lips peeled back, and he growled through clenched teeth.

II

"If you try anything stupid," Baker said as he led me down a dim hallway, "we'll shoot your wife and sister. I already told them that if they act up, we'll shoot you."

"Better hope they like me," I replied.

The hallway opened onto a large dining room, the kind I had seen only in movies: a narrow table ran its length, its red tablecloth burdened with silver platters and burning candles in gracefully curved holders, along with buckets filled with ice, beer, and bottles of high-end whiskey. A fireplace burned at the far end, its flickering light glinting off the herd of stag heads on the walls. Whoever owned this place was a real hunter, or pretended to be. Baker swept out an arm, gesturing for me to sit in one of the plush chairs beside the table.

"Gee, is all this for me?" I said. "How kind of you. We don't get out to dinner that often. Expensive, you know."

Pressing a hand against my spine, Varney shoved me forward.

"No, that food is for our guests," Baker said. "But don't worry, we'll pack some calories in you before the main event. You'll need 'em."

That sounded menacing. I sat in the offered chair. The setting had a nice china plate, two crystal glasses, and three or four more forks and spoons than I thought necessary to eat a meal. There was also a nice, sharp knife for cutting meat.

Varney reached into a pocket and tossed an energy bar on my plate. Beneath the faint scent of burning wood I smelled meat and spices cooking somewhere in the house, and my stomach rumbled. Locking eyes with Varney, I dropped the energy bar on the floor.

"You'll regret that," Varney said.

"Boys, stop." Baker had taken a seat across from us. "Send them in."

Every nerve in Varney's body wanted to slap me across the face. I added a smile to my stare down. "Go on," I said. "Serve your master."

The blood drained from his face.

"Good doggie," I cooed.

"Varney," Baker said, louder.

Turning on his heel, Varney ripped open a door behind us. Janine slid into the chair to my left, trembling but unmarked. Frankie plopped into the chair to my right, a massive bruise darkening her cheekbone, her cheeks flaring with a rage hotter than the nearby fire.

I reached out and gripped my wife's hand. She squeezed back, hard enough to grind my bones.

"One big happy family," Baker said, sweeping his hands wide.

"Why don't you cut the shit," Frankie said, "and tell us why we're here?" She plucked a beer from the nearest bucket, popped the tab, and downed half of it in one swallow.

Behind me, Varney snarled deep in his throat.

Baker raised a hand. "It's okay."

"Better curb that doggie." I smirked and freed two beers from the ice, handing one to Janine. No way they would shoot us here, with guests inbound. It takes a lot of time to clean brains and blood off silver and china.

"You'll regret that beer," Baker said. "We'd like you to keep your wits about you. Makes things more fun."

"Uh-oh, scary," I said.

Baker laughed. It was fake amusement. I could tell because big drops of sweat had formed on his forehead. Despite the fire roaring a few feet away, the central air kept the room nice and cool. If he was sweating like bin Laden at a firefighter convention, it was probably because my family refused to cower and cry along with the twisted script in his head.

"I know you," Frankie said. "You're Ted Baker. You're the richest man in the state."

"No wonder I don't recognize him," I said. "I don't know anyone rich." I liked playing a redneck who never read the news. Baker owned a local fast-food chain, famous for its fried chicken and regular violation of labor laws. He owned a huge mansion on the north side of Boise, on the same ridge as the potato kings and microchip executives and other captains of industry. We were probably inside that house.

"Why are we here?" Frankie drained her beer and crumpled the can against the table, denting the wood. "To what do we owe the pleasure?"

"Your father," Baker said.

"Excuse me?" I asked.

Baker yanked a bottle of whiskey from a bucket, pulled free the cork, and filled a nearby glass. "Thirty years ago," he said. "Reagan's War on Drugs is picking up, but that's not stopping all the profit flowing over the border. Your dad gets in a little dispute with a couple of Mexicans carrying ten kilos in their car..."

"We remember," Frankie said, glancing at me.

Baker shook his head, hard, like a dog breaking a rat in its jaws. "With all due respect, no, you don't. Because if you knew what actually happened that afternoon, you'd dig up your dead dad and spit right in his eye."

I helped myself to another beer. If I was about to die, I might as well depart this world with a buzz. "I doubt I'd do anything of the kind, but explain," I said.

"You remember your dad's partner, giant of a guy, red-head with a big ol' porn moustache? His name was John, John..."

"Benson," Frankie said.

"Benson, that's it. Benson was crooked as a dog's hind leg, and he had a deal with those Mexicans to give them secure passage for their shit. He wanted to cut your father in on it, not because he was a nice guy, but because..."

"If you're crooked, having an honest partner just doesn't work," Frankie said. "Rules of the game."

"Exactly. Smarter than you look, girl. And your father, the dumbass, instead of just taking the money, decides to play cowboy. Thought he'd arrest everyone, make a name for himself. Well, Benson and those boys from Mexico had other ideas. There was a shootout."

"My father killed them all," I said. "He turned the coke in, but it disappeared in custody."

"He did, and it did. That coke was supposed to go to my brother, Robert, who was a bit of a dealer back then. And when that coke didn't arrive, what do you think happened?"

I shrugged. "Everybody said, 'Shit happens,' and moved on?"

Baker took a deep sip of whiskey. "Robert, God rest his soul, was not the brightest mind this family ever produced. He owed some bad people a lot of money, which the coke deal would've covered. I wasn't as big then as I am now, so I couldn't help him out, although Lord knows I tried. And you probably know the rest."

"Sorry," Janine said. "We haven't kept up with your illustrious family history."

"Someone came up behind my brother in his driveway and bashed his brains out." Baker drained his glass. "Didn't kill him at first, but he was in a coma for three years before he finally went to his great reward. Is your father the only one to blame here? He is not. But you better believe that whenever we've needed a new player for our little game, your name was always near the top of my list."

"What little game?" Frankie asked.

Baker waved the empty glass back and forth. "I'm going to savor this. The thought of taking out your bloodline, it gives me a bit of a woody, I'm not afraid to admit."

"What little game?" Frankie asked again, louder.

"You got a tough gang, I heard?" Baker squinted at her. "I got a tougher one. It's called the state government, and the cops, and friends in Washington. They look like a bunch of fat white men, but trust me when I tell you they can fuck up your shit better than anyone, because they can do it in broad daylight without worrying about any consequences."

I raised my hand like an anxious kid in class. "I have a big question."

Baker's attention shifted. "What's that, son?"

"Do you rehearse speeches like that in the mirror?" I wanted to see how much I could irritate him. "Because you had it down. I'm serious. It was like watching a movie, with all your pauses and emphasizing certain words. Do me a favor? Stick your hands out like you're holding an Oscar and say, 'I'd like to thank the Academy.'"

"You're going to be a lot less funny out on the course," Baker said.

"What's the game?" Janine asked.

"You'll see," Baker said, reaching again for the whiskey. "You'll see."

"Well, I need more alcohol if I'm going to listen to more of this bullshit," Frankie said, plucking the nearest bottle. Turning it to examine the label, she declared: "Fifteen years aged. Usually I don't drink anything less than thirty years. What do you have to say about that, Varney?"

"I don't have an opinion," Varney said.

Frankie tilted the bottle to reveal the label, before peeling back the shrink-wrapped plastic around the cap with the edge of a nail. I braced my heels against the floor, gripped the chair's plush arms, and traded a look with Janine.

Frankie smiled sweetly at Baker. "I do have one other question."

Baker paused in mid-pour. "What is it?" he asked.

"What made you such an asshole?" she said, and, without waiting for a reply, gripped the bottle by the neck, spun in her seat, and tossed it overhand at Varney. She had maybe a quarter-second to aim but her reflexes were true and the bottle smacked him in the forehead. Varney yelped. The bottle thumped unbroken to the floorboards.

Before Varney could draw his weapon, Frankie jumped from her seat and plowed a boot into his stomach, slamming him into the wall. On the far side of the table, Baker shoved his chair back and stood on wavering legs, gasping in surprise. It would have taken me a two-week journey on camelback to walk around a table that big, so I decided to leap on top of it, my feet knocking aside silver platters and buckets as I rushed him.

Baker was too stunned to run. I dropped onto him, my knees driving his stomach into his spine, his breath blasting from his lungs with a loud whoosh. He fell into his seat, which cracked. While he struggled to suck down air, I climbed off him and grabbed the nearest sharp knife, glancing at the action across the table as I did so.

Janine leapt from her chair and sprinted at Varney, who swung a wild fist at Frankie's head. Frankie dodged, stepped back, and tried to rabbit-punch Varney in the throat, but he raised a hand to block it. He was getting over his initial surprise. Janine, who had taken a couple of self-defense classes at the local gym and spent most of her life around me, went low, aiming a kick at his knees. Varney fell, and Frankie and Janine whaled on him with the passion of a couple of officers at a traffic stop gone wrong.

I stepped behind Baker, slotted my arm around his throat, and hauled him upright, the tip of the blade pressed hard against his jugular. "I have no problem with bleeding a rich pig," I told him, "but you're more useful to me alive."

Frankie retrieved Varney's pistol and slotted it against his bloody temple, finger on the trigger, other hand raised in anticipation of the splatter.

"No shots," I said. "Might be other people in the house."

"Like we haven't made noise already." Frankie laughed.

"There are lots of other people here," Baker said. "I'll make you a deal: let me go, drop your weapons, and you get to play the game. Try to get away, and we will kill you all."

"We'll take our chances on Option B," I said, pressing the knife deeper into his flesh. "Now which way do we go out? Remember: you mess with us, you're the one who's dying first."

As blood trickled down his neck, soaking his collar, Baker nodded toward the doorway on our left.

"Let's go," I said, shoving him in that direction. Walking with a hostage is always hard if they refuse to play along, but Baker put some pep in his step. I had to yank his elbow to make him slow down a little.

After kicking Varney one final time in the back of the head, Frankie followed in my wake, Janine beside her. In that smaller trophy room where Varney had first removed my hood, we found the corgi splayed on its back, its tongue lolling. At least someone was having a relaxing night around here.

"Where now?" I asked Baker.

"There's just one door, you idiot," he said, nodding to his right.

Frankie placed an ear against the wood, listening for several heartbeats before turning the knob. She stood back so Baker could enter first. We crossed into a long corridor painted white, lined with fluorescent lights that cast our skin in corpse-like hues: a service corridor. I hoped it led outside.

Midway down the corridor, we passed a pair of swinging doors with portholes set at eye-level. Through the smeared glass I saw chefs in white bustling around an industrial kitchen, clanging pots as greasy flames burst from a massive range. On a table at the center of the chaos sat a roasted pig.

We moved on, toward the gunmetal-gray door at the end of the corridor, where a red EXIT sign promised freedom. "Stay calm," I muttered in Baker's ear. Edging him slightly to my left, I kicked my right foot against the push bar.

The door creaked open, a cool rush of night air washing over us.

We stepped outside, clustered tight behind Baker, ready for anything.

What I saw next stopped me cold.

Behind me, Frankie and Janine gasped.

In front of us stood a man in a green mesh vest and camouflage hunting fatigues and maroon boots that looked new and expensive. I recognized the blue eyes and imperial nose: U.S. Senator Ted Ryan, big on slashing social services and tax cuts, bigger on preaching morality at every opportunity. He appeared unarmed, an empty holster on his left hip.

He stood in the middle of a gravel lot that curved along the flattened top of a steep hillside. Above us, blazing with light, loomed Baker's house—a monstrosity of logs and domed roofs and picture windows, like a Great Hall in a Tolkien epic. A porch ran its length, and on it stood maybe a dozen men.

Like Varney, they wore black tactical gear. They held rifles and shotguns pointed in our direction, breeches closed and magazines slotted. I saw enough long beards and cool gazes to know I had once fought alongside guys like this, hardened by endless tours in nowhere deserts.

Baker made a sound deep in his throat. At first I thought it was a cough, or maybe a pain noise, but it continued. He was laughing.

"You best put that knife down," called one of the men

on the porch.

Ted Ryan, the honorable gentleman from the Great State of Idaho, celebrated speaker, noted humanitarian, said: "What the fuck is this?"

"This is us walking out of here," I said, trying to put as much force in my voice as possible. At the edge of the lot sat a row of mud-splattered SUVs and trucks. Maybe one had keys in the ignition. A guy could hope, right?

Baker gurgle-giggled again, louder.

"Why don't you put your weapons down, and we can talk about this?" Ryan held his hands high, palms out. "I'm sure it's all a misunderstanding."

Frankie laughed and raised Varney's pistol an inch: "Misunderstanding, my ass."

"Anyone does anything, this guy dies," I announced, loud enough for my voice to echo into the night. I felt Baker's pulse whispering through the knife's handle. A little more pressure and I would cut something serious.

"If you kill him, then you all die. So I guess we have a little bit of a standoff on our hands, don't we?" Ryan glanced at Baker, reading something in his expression. "We'll make you a deal."

"What?" Janine asked.

"Set the weapons down, and play the game," Ryan said. "People have lived through it before. Truly. You might make a lot of money from it. We're not too worried about you telling the authorities, because, well." He swept out an arm over the men, the vehicles, the enormous house, the state he had helped govern for fifteen years.

"Bullshit," Frankie sang.

Ryan shrugged. He made the same gesture on television whenever he announced a budget impasse. It was so surreal, watching this famous man try to negotiate me down from killing another famous man that I briefly wondered whether this whole thing was a hallucination. Maybe that crazed Viking at the trailer park had buried his axe in my skull, and my dying brain was trying to deal with that fact by spinning up an elaborate fantasy of politicians and gunmen.

The gravel exploded at Janine's feet. A shot echoed over the hills.

On the porch, bloody Varney had a smoking rifle socked to his shoulder.

Frankie raised her pistol, and a second shot snapped over her head.

"I wouldn't," Ryan said, shaking his head.

They would kill us all. We weren't human to them.

I lowered the knife and Baker stumbled away, rubbing his throat. I gave him three feet before I planted a swift kick in his ass, sending him crashing to the gravel. One of the mercenaries on the porch laughed. I would probably pay for that later, but damn if it didn't feel good right now.

Frankie dropped her pistol and presented both middle fingers. Three of the men on the porch covered us with rifles as the rest made their way down the stairs.

"I'm sorry," I told my wife, before a hulking dude with a long gray beard slammed his rifle stock into my jaw.

III

I awoke.

Darkness.

The hood. I was back in that damn hood again.

My jaw ached. Cold drool on my chin. I jabbed a tongue into my teeth, probing for any loose ones, relieved when everything felt normal.

I listened as best I could through the thick cloth. The truck rumbled around me. Distant honking. A relaxed hand on my shoulder held me upright. I moved my wrists and metal bit the skin. Handcuffs. The truck leaned into a curve, and warmth spread along my shoulder and the side of my head—sunlight. Maybe it was dawn. Were Janine and Frankie in here with me?

I thought about calling out and decided against it.

The truck took more turns that made my body sway back and forth. No sounds of other cars, and after a few minutes I gave up trying to guess our location. Instead I found myself thinking about my last will and testament, or lack thereof. The kid would get everything, of course, and there was enough money in our accounts to maybe buy her a year of college, if nobody touched it for ten years. That was something of a relief. Except.

Except.

Except they might never find our bodies.

No bodies, no investigation, right? If they tossed us in the woods, it might take years for a hunter to find the bones, if ever. And that wasn't even the worst part. These men were smart and cautious, the kind who clipped their loose ends.

They might kill my whole family.

That thought, combined with the swaying of the truck, made my stomach churn. When was the last time I'd been this scared? Maybe Iraq, on the day I splattered that Baghdad boy's head. Vomit crawled up my throat, and I swallowed in a failing attempt to hold it back.

Before I could coat the inside of the hood with my stomach, the truck screeched to a stop. A door creaked open, and hands grabbed me beneath the armpits. Hot air on my arms and face. My knees hit rocky ground, sharp enough to make me wince. Birds chirped. Water roared.

The handcuffs popped free.

Someone yanked the hood away.

I knelt on a long slope of loose red gravel, dotted with patches of wild yellow grass. Far below, the angle steepened into the rushing blackness of a narrow river. Further downstream, the gravelly slopes rose into sheer granite cliffs, studded with the scraggly pine trees that endure for decades in harsh conditions.

Looking upstream, I saw dense forest above the slopes and the river; and rising beyond the trees, a tall ridge of barren and unforgiving rock.

"You recognize this place?" Varney asked. He stood to my left, forcing me to turn my hips to see him better. He still wore his black garb, including the vest, and a small backpack. A blood-spotted bandage covered the bridge of his nose, and a nasty bruise bloomed on his left cheek. Frankie and Janine had given him a wonderful beating.

"No," I said.

"Ore Valley," he said. "Flat-out middle of nowhere. We used to do this thing closer in, but after those two kids... better safe than sorry, you know what I mean?"

"Whatever." I knew the valley by reputation. The whole area had a century of bad luck under its belt: mining cave-ins, toxic leaks, drinking water with enough lead in it to turn children into paperweights. Over a thousand people once lived in the town beside the mining works. The state had evacuated them all when it figured out the local life expectancy had plunged to medieval levels.

"Baker bought the whole acreage," Varney continued. "Promised some pansy environmental group he would clean up the soil and water, turn it into a park or some shit. Real funny, huh?"

"Yeah," I offered in my most deadpan voice. "That's a real gut-buster."

Varney's face reddened. He drew his pistol and, bending down, jammed it hard against my thigh. "Give me a reason," he said.

I smiled, trying to ignore the acid burning my throat. "Baker won't like that. It'll make the game less entertaining if I'm limping around. Where are my people?"

Varney ground the barrel hard into the muscle before slipping the weapon back into its holster. "They're close," he said.

Loose gravel trickled past me. I twisted around to see a man walking toward us. He came from the same stock as Varney—tall, thin, with that sun-blasted skin of men who spend their lives outside without the benefit of hat or sunscreen. The top of his balding head was flecked with pink-ish spots that looked like prime candidates for skin cancer. Unlike Varney in his black hunting garb, this one wore jeans and a button-down blue shirt, along with a six-shooter in a leather holster on his hip. A tattoo darkened the back of his left wrist: an iron cross.

"Who are you?" I asked him.

"Fred," he said.

"Fred who?"

"Fred gonna shoot your ass dead, you keep talking," Varney said. "Now sit back and stick your leg out. Doesn't matter which one."

I refused to move. Varney placed a hand on his pistol. I stuck out a single leg and grinned. I calculated my chances if I pushed off and sledded that rough gravel all the way to the water: zero. Either of these men would blast my head off before I reached the river. And where would that leave Frankie and Janine?

Varney unslung his backpack, unzipped it, and drew out a handful of nylon and canvas. Turning to Fred, he said: "If he moves, kill him."

Fred nodded and drew his pistol, a .357 revolver. Bend-ing down, Varney untangled the mass in his hand until it resolved into a loop of well-worn canvas and wires, con-nected to a black plastic box the size of a pack of ciga-rettes. Varney wrapped the loop tight around my right leg, just beneath the calf, and pressed a button on the side of the box.

"That's a modified shock collar." Varney patted my leg and stood up. "You know how pooch gets too close to the edge of the yard, the collar gives them a little zap? You walk over the property line, the circuit in the band sets off the couple ounces of plastic explosive in the lining there. Blast your leg clean off, and you bleed to death."

I lifted my leg to examine the loop. A tiny light on the box burned red as a demon's eye. "You're such a charmer," I said.

Varney ignored my quip. "If you're thinking you can somehow get it off, don't. You tamper with it, it blows. You can blame those two kids. If they hadn't gotten so far away from the hunting grounds, we wouldn't have needed to build this. It's an improvised piece of shit, but it works, believe me."

Varney neglected to mention the most important part, which is that two teenagers had managed to escape several armed men and almost make it to freedom. That boy must have thought all his troubles were over when he spotted the bright beacon of the Quik-Stop, and its promise of a phone and living witnesses. That girl had lost her clothes and taken a bullet to the side but kept running anyway. Good for them.

"The Quik-Stop," I said. "Was that you?"

Varney nodded, pursing his lips.

"How about the girl?" I asked.

"One of our guests got a shot off with a .22." Varney sighed. "The guy thought he was a real pro, chose a small gun because he wanted to keep things 'challenging,' he said. We knew we hit her, but she fell in the river. Took me forever to find the body. Guess what we did after that?"

"Why don't you tell me, man?"

Varney smiled, his gaze distant, as if reliving a happy memory. "We put her in your house. Waited until you left, then walked right in and stuffed her in that big gun safe. We wanted to fuck with you. Give you a taste of what was coming, even if you didn't know it yet."

"Did she have a necklace?"

"What?"

"A little silver thing. I found it outside, near the fence."

He shrugged. "If you'd walked fifteen feet into that brush, you might have found her. We hid her there, waiting until you and your wife left. That jewelry must have fallen off at some point."

I worked things out in my head. "When you pulled me over, that wasn't a coincidence."

"No, sir. I'd been tracking you for an hour by that point. If that cover hadn't flown off your boat, I would've stopped you anyway. I wanted to look in your eyes."

"You must feel so proud of yourself," I said. "Killing kids. How much they pay you? Is it worth it?"

Varney turned away, plunging a hand into his backpack. "You think you're smart, don't you? You and your sister," he called over his shoulder. "You know we left that phone in the field, right? Figured you'd track it down. The second you pinged it, we got our team ready, set up a nice little ambush. How's that feel?"

"I've seen Iraqi teenagers put on better ambushes," I told him. "No joke."

From the backpack Varney drew a fat digital watch, which he tossed on the gravel beside my legs. "Put this on," he said. "Typical model, ten bucks, nothing fancy. Our little gift to you."

"My rifle you took?" I said. "How about you give it back? Even the odds a little."

Varney nodded to the south. "Pay attention."

Beside the river, at the base of the granite cliffs, the land flattened into a stony beach. A sleek black jeep crunched to a stop on the water's edge, its doors opening to dispense men in black suits and white shirts. They looked like waiters. Two opened the trunk and removed a large wicker picnic basket, along with a folding table and a tablecloth.

Moving with the precise movements of professionals, they unfolded the table, covered it with the tablecloth, and set the basket atop it as an anchor against the stiff breeze. One opened the basket and reached inside, removing two bottles of champagne and eight glasses.

"Fancy," I said.

"Shut your mouth," Varney shot back.

Their task completed, the men stood at attention beside the table, hands clasped behind their backs. Two luxury SUVs rolled into view, black flanks spotted with mud, and stopped behind the jeep. Nine men climbed out: white, middle-aged, and fit in that way of those who can afford personal trainers and watch what they eat. All had shaven-clean heads or newscaster hair. One of them was my good buddy Baker. Another was Senator Ryan.

Baker walked over to the table, uncorked the champagne, and filled the glasses. Over the roar of the river I heard the men chattering and laughing. The waiters walked to the SUVs and opened the trunks, retrieving several black and green rifle cases.

It was an upscale hunting party. As Baker passed around the glasses of champagne, he launched into a spiel. Over the roaring river I caught the words "welfare" and "deadbeat," followed by "drinking problem." When he turned and pointed in my direction, and the men around him laughed, I knew he was talking about me.

"I got a job," I said. "I'm not a deadbeat." A small, wounded part of me needed to voice that. Out of all the

things that had happened to me over the past day or so—
injured, kidnapped, placed at the center of this sick little
game—somehow this hurt the worst. I had done my best
to make something of myself in this world, whatever my
mistakes.

"Shut up," Varney said.

I studied the men in the crowd, recognizing three of
them. Furthest to the left stood Bret Olson, the former
governor of our fair state, a silver fox of a man decked out
like a duck hunter in camo and a beige hunting vest. He
became famous during his second term for signing a strict
anti-gay bill into law—a week before a reporter caught
him making out with his press secretary, a handsome former basketball star named John Hemingway. Olson re-
signed soon after that, claiming he needed to spend more
time with his family.

Olson stood next to a guy so muscular that, from this
distance, he looked like a half-pound of rocks squeezed
into a condom. In contrast to the other men decked out in
hunting gear, this steroid-happy gentleman wore a tight T-
shirt, the better to show off the meat, and a pair of cargo
pants. I knew the face: Jim Marshall, whose lawyers had
pled "affluenza" when his son Stephen crashed a truck into
Scott Parson's minivan. As best I could recall from the
news reports, Jim had made a fortune screwing people
over in real estate. You could argue that his actions had
led to Parson sprawled on the ground behind his house,
wheezing that he had a job to do. I felt a stab of regret. I
should have let Parson have his shot.

Shifting away from Marshall, my gaze fell on the next
man in the group: Rob, my next-door neighbor, dressed in
new hunting clothes and a bright orange cap. Even from

halfway up the valley I could read the tension in his frown, and the hunch of his shoulders. I offered a thumbs-up, hoping he could see it. He knew me as a human being, as opposed to prey, and that might make him hesitate when it came time to pull the trigger. Lord knows how he ended up in this crew of predators.

Baker concluded his little speech. The men raised their glasses in unison and hollered something lost in the rumble of wind. They drank.

"On your feet," Varney said, gripping my collar. "You got a race to run."

"Where's the finish line?" I asked, letting him help me upright. "How do we win?"

"Just got to outlast them," he said vaguely.

I knew they intended to kill us, of course. It was that lack of masks.

I considered the pros and cons of hitting Varney in the face. If I took him down, grabbed his gun, and shot Fred, I would buy myself time to find my family and kill every one of those fuckers down below. But knocking Varney over depended on everything going right, and if my life had proven anything, it's when you need everything to go right that it all twists horribly wrong.

As if reading my thoughts, Fred raised his .357 and said: "Folks tried that before. Didn't make it."

"Maybe they weren't me."

"Maybe they were better."

From his pack, Varney drew a plastic canteen with a black nylon strap and tossed it to me. I snatched it out of the air and shook it, guessing from the sloshing that it was roughly half-full. That would last me no time at all, unless I refilled it from one of the valley's famous toxic rivers.

Things were looking better and better.

"They're going to fire off a round down below," Varney said, nodding to the group. "When that happens, you got your opportunity to run. I advise you head into those woods there."

The hunters retrieved their rifles and loaded up, filling their vest pockets with spare rounds. They looked like any ordinary group of men readying for a long day of hunting deer. One of them laughed and slapped another on the back.

"Where are my people?" I asked, slinging the canteen over my shoulder.

Varney pointed to the far side of the valley. In the shadow of a scraggly pine, on a platform of gray rock, I saw a trio of small dark shapes. It was hard to tell much more from this distance. "They got the same orders as you," Varney said. "Run. And remember: there's always a chance you might live."

"You missed your true calling," I said, "writing those inspirational cards. You know, the ones you find in the drug store?" My voice dipped low: "'There's a chance you might live.'" I shifted back to my regular tone. "We could put an image of a cute kitten over it."

He wanted to hit me. I could tell by the way his hand flexed on his weapon. Something held him back. He probably had orders not to ruin the prey before paying clients had a shot at it.

"Those two kids got away," I said. "They weren't trained, but they did their best. I'm betting it can be done again."

"We'll see," Varney said, and waved his pistol at a dirt track that led up the slope to the woods. "Like I said, head toward the forest. Trust me when I tell you we could end this little game in five minutes, put a bullet in you from a hundred yards away. We know this land that well. But everyone's paying for a show, so we'll drag it out a bit."

"If you got some peace to make," added Fred, "best make it in your head."

"Thanks, Marlboro Nazi," I said. "Why don't you go screw yourself?"

Fred bent and spat in the dust. "Get going. If you're quick, you might link up with your women."

I took a step toward the woods, my heart hammering, my head too light. The adrenaline in my blood since last night had soured, leaving me sick. Far below, the hunters paused in their conversation, their heads swiveling after me. Their stares made me feel too fat, too huge, too full of fluids held in place only by the thinnest of skins. I prayed that my neighbor Rob had a conscience, because I would need all the help I could get out here.

Forcing those thoughts aside, I started to run, not looking back, expecting to hear the loud crack of a bullet and a brief flash of pain before everything went dark. Or maybe bullets moved so fast you died before you ever heard the shot, plunging you into nonexistence seamlessly as a movie's cut to the end credits. Not a comforting thought. The explosive loop made one leg a little heavier than the other, throwing off my stride on the loose gravel as I veered for the comforting black beneath the pines.

Running through the woods, I tried to recall everything I had ever heard about Ore Valley, in hopes of orienting myself a little bit. I knew that beyond the woods and the ridge, the land flattened into a dusty basin where the miners and their families had set up a town in the old days, a few miles from the massive smelter where they extracted silver from rock. Over the ensuing decades, the basin had developed a reputation as a den of sin where a hundred dollars could buy you a blackout night and a nice case of syphilis.

Back in the day, my uncles and father would talk about all the truckers who stopped off in Ore Valley to blow their paychecks, and that, combined with the mining companies' need to take whatever they blasted from the mountains to the broader world, made me think the highway was close to the town. That was good to know, but nothing I could use until I figured out how to pry this bomb off my leg.

I paused beside an elm to catch my breath, dismayed at how my breathing already felt shot. My fingers skimmed the black box, the sun-warmed canvas and wires. Was it fake? I couldn't take the chance of pulling a wire to see what happened. Varney struck me as someone who didn't bluff.

I took a sip of water from the canteen, swallowed, and held my breath, listening for any sounds above the rustling of the wind through the dry branches. Nothing. Those bastards by the river were probably still finishing their drinks.

I needed to find Frankie and Janine, first. Frankie might have a plan already. At the very least, we would make these assholes sing for their supper.

I took another deep breath and held it, willing my heart to slow. When I felt a little calmer, I started through the woods, pausing every few minutes to peer at the sun and orient myself in the direction of the ridge where I had last seen my sister and wife. At one point I passed a massive boulder worn jagged by millions of years of weather and stopped long enough to pick a loose shard of rock from its base. Its sharp edge would prove next to useless against a gun, but I might get lucky.

A rifle-shot echoed through the woods. The hunt was officially on.

I ran, keeping to a pace that let me breathe easy. Sweat made my neck itch, and I felt my pulse in my fingers. If we made it out of this alive, I would rededicate myself to an exercise regimen more vigorous than tackling the occasional felon. Just ahead, the pine woods fell away before a sun-dappled clearing, overgrown with weeds. In the middle of the clearing sat a huge shed that had seen better years: its roof collapsing, its red-painted sides flaked rougher than alligator skin.

Someone with a sense of humor had padlocked the shed's main door. Raising my rock, I brought it down hard on the rotted wood bolted to the hasp, sending the lock clattering to the dust. I pushed the door open onto darkness, crouching low. There was no way a hunter could have looped in front of me this quickly, unless they had taken an SUV, and I would have heard the engine. Nonetheless, I ducked through the doorway quietly as I could.

Dusty shafts of light stabbed from holes in the ceiling, illuminating huge, mold-spotted tarps over hulks. I lifted the edge of the closest one, seeing rusty metal, gears, a chain. Mining equipment of some sort, left here to rust after everything in the area shut down.

I considered ducking under one of these tarps, going to ground like a varmint. Bad idea. If none of the hunters found me, which seemed unlikely, Frankie and Janine still needed my help. Besides, that black box on my leg maybe had a tracker in it, ready to scream my location if the hunters got too frustrated.

I heard a faint rattle.

You think the phrase "every hair standing on end" is a cliché until a rattlesnake shakes its ass near you, and you realize just how effectively humans are programmed to run away from anything with poison and teeth.

I leapt back from the tarp-covered machine, and as I did, I swear I saw a shadow slither into deeper darkness. For all I knew, there was a whole nest of creepy-crawly beasties in there.

Beating a hasty retreat to the door, I passed a board of rusty, cobweb-smeared tools on the wall. With a little bit of ingenuity, of course, anything with a halfway-decent edge or a bit of weight can serve as a weapon, so I decided to check out the selection. Most of the tools—a screwdriver, a pair of pliers—were too small for anything other than close-in work, but hanging from the largest nail was a heavy wrecking bar with a rocker head. It looked like a pry bar on steroids. Hefting it made me feel a little bit better about our chances.

Whistling a tune to myself, swinging that bar like a baseball star warming up for the first inning, I headed out the door.

IV

I cut through the woods toward the river. Although I hoped that Janine and Frankie would head south, in my direction, I had no way of communicating with them. I suspected the hunters would move slow and loud, and that might create excellent opportunities for an ambush.

The land rose at a steep angle, forcing me to scrabble sideways while using the wrecking bar as a makeshift cane. My calves already ached—a bad sign—and my sweaty shirt clung to my chest. Through the trees I sighted the ridge where I had seen Frankie and Janine. Maybe they were close.

I heard a low thud ahead, too soft for a gunshot. It sounded like a watermelon hit with a hammer. As I crept forward, cautious, the brush in front of me rustled, and a pale face flickered behind a ragged granite formation that looked like a dragon's tooth. Relief flooded through me, so warm and strong it felt almost like morphine: it was Janine, her forehead notched with dark cuts but otherwise okay.

She disappeared, and I scrambled around the boulder, my shoes slipping on moist leaves. The granite splattered dark. I smelled wet pennies, raw meat. Frankie knelt atop a hunter in an orange vest, her arms moving with industrial force as she brought down a rock again and again on a red

150

mess that had once been a face.

Janine stood with her hand over her mouth. I set my wrecking bar against the rock and hugged her tight, burying my face in her hair, breathing deep her sweet scent. It crowded out the copper stink of blood.

"Kelly," she said, through her fingers, transfixed by the sight of Frankie converting a hunter to ground beef.

"We're going to get out of this," I whispered into her neck. "And then we're going to go get her, okay?"

Janine wiped her eyes. "Your mom won't let her go."

"Then I'll have to use the taser," I said, and she laughed. I felt a little better, strong enough to turn and face my sister's handiwork. Growling deep in her throat like a cornered animal, Frankie tossed aside the dripping rock and proceeded to ransack the corpse's pockets, which yielded a small yellow radio and a set of keys with a BMW fob.

Both women had loops of canvas and wiring around their lower legs. My relief curdled to dread. In Baghdad, I had seen a few people turned into suicide bombers against their will, wired up with explosives and forced to walk toward a patrol, crying and screaming as we yelled at them to stop, fuck you, stop. They must have felt the same terror as I did at that moment.

Janine kicked aside some leaves near our feet, revealing the hunter's weapon: a fancy Kel-Tec KSG pump-action, with a pair of tube magazines beneath the barrel. Looked brand new, and I wondered if the poor sucker had ever fired it before Frankie went Neanderthal on his chunky ass.

Frankie turned to me, her face flecked with red. "Take a look," she said, handing over the man's wallet. I flipped open the billfold to study the driver's license. The name John Patterson was unfamiliar, but the photograph I recognized from a highway billboard near the exit to our house: John the Barbarian, the Shock-Jock Screamer of Treasure Valley Talk Radio, infamous for making jokes about school shootings and incest. As far as I was concerned, Frankie had just done the human race a service.

"Never whacked a celebrity," Frankie said.

Handing my iron bar to Janine, I lifted the shotgun and aimed it downhill. "He alone?"

"Yeah, came charging ahead, breathing hard," Janine said. "Excited, I guess. He didn't see Frankie before she jumped him."

"Give me the gun." Frankie held out a hand.

"Why?" I asked.

"Because I killed him. It's my trophy. You get the radio."

She had a point. Growing up in our house, you got to keep whatever you captured or killed. And although I hated to admit it, Frankie was a much better shot, and had probably killed more people over the years, even when you took my time overseas into account. I tossed her the weapon, and took the radio in return, which I handed to Janine. With both hands free, I could better use my wrecking bar.

"Where are we going?" Janine whispered.

That was an excellent question. We needed space and time to puzzle out how to snip these bombs off our legs without setting off the explosives. Then we had to kill everyone in the vicinity and call for help. And even if we got our hands on a phone, who were the good guys in this situation? The most powerful people in the state wanted to mount our heads on their trophy walls.

"There's cover," I said, nodding in the direction I'd come from. "A shed."

Frankie snorted. "There's a whole town over the ridge behind us."

I squinted at her. "You been there?"

"Did some deals here, a long time ago," she said. "Nothing like an abandoned area to exchange a ton of weapons, you know? Even the meth cookers won't set up out here, it's too remote. Anyway, that shed or whatever is a bad idea. I bet some of these dudes have longer-range rifles. We stay in the woods, we're dead meat."

As if on cue, we heard a distant shouting from down-slope. A blue shape darted between trees. The radio in Janine's hand came alive, crackling and spitting, and she twisted it off, but not before a second voice called out.

Oh shit, I thought. Here we go.

Frankie and Janine picked their way upslope through the trees. I retrieved my wrecking bar and headed after them, hoping that the sight of the mauled corpse would distract our pursuers for a few minutes.

V

On the far side of the ridge, we came in sight of the town. An empty road ran through it, the black asphalt crumbling to sand and gravel in patches. The sun blazed down on a small cluster of buildings at the main intersection, weathered and beaten-down, the edifices held together with peeling paint; it flashed on the swaying metal sign of the gas station at the bottom of the hill.

The slope had large slabs of rock baking in the heat. Anyone on the ridge would have a decent shot at us if we tried to make our way across those. I pointed to our right, where erosion had split two of the slabs apart, leaving a narrow channel thick with bushes. I wasn't anxious for another encounter with a rattler, but the idea of snakes underfoot won out over a bullet in the back of the head.

I went first, using my bar to crush the brush in front of us. My boots crunched over sticks and dead brush, but no poisonous reptiles. Janine followed me, her hand on my shoulder, while Frankie brought up the rear, pausing every minute or so to swivel around and check our flank. The shotgun sank in her grip, and I could feel my own arms beginning to ache. Carrying weapons is a real workout, as any soldier will tell you.

The drainage channel opened onto the road, with no

cover until we reached the first buildings on the far side. We angled toward the gas station and the shade of its far wall, which would provide some cover from the ridge. Fright made my throat clench so hard it felt like breathing through a cocktail straw. The bullet could come at any time. The ridgeline, hairy with trees and backlit by the sun, was the ultimate hunting blind.

While we paused for breath against that cool wall, Janine pointed at the bombs on our ankles. "What do we do about these?"

I wanted to tell her something, anything. "I don't think they'll detonate them unless they have to. It'll ruin their little game."

"Comforting," Frankie said, gesturing for Janine to try the radio. "I got a plan for dealing with it, but you're not going to like it at all."

Janine twisted the dial on the radio. It spat static, no voices.

"Your people," I asked her. "They'll know you're missing at some point, right? How long until the cavalry finds us?"

"That's assuming they have any idea where we are," she said. "I wouldn't hold out hope, buddy. We might be on our own."

"Then we need to buy ourselves a little space. Hard to figure out what to do with these guys breathing down our necks." I took a swig from my canteen and passed it to Janine, who sipped and handed it over to Frankie. We needed more water. The heat and the fear reminded me so much of Iraq I could almost smell the chemical shit burning in the fields. I risked a peek around the corner of the building, toward the ridge. No movement, aside from the wind stirring the tops of the tallest trees.

"How about there?" Janine giggled, a hand over her mouth.

Frankie barked laughter, loud, and pointed across the road.

At the edge of a baking expanse of parking lot, a fading billboard proclaimed BIG FUN AT THE CLOWN MOTEL! in bulging balloon letters. Above the words loomed a giant clown with a shark's grin and a shaved head, juggling a variety of colored balls.

Beyond the billboard stood a two-story motel, shaped in a horseshoe around a broken concrete courtyard, the doors on the second floor opening onto a wraparound balcony. It looked like so many other cockroach havens you found on the highways and byways of America, except for the clown-white walls and the brightly colored railings. It gleamed in the sun like a child's nightmare.

"Oh yeah," Frankie said. "I forgot about this place. Or more like, blocked it out of my memory, because, you know, clowns."

"Who the hell designed it?" Janine asked. "Stephen King?"

"Freakiness aside," Frankie said. "It's a good place to hide out. With that many rooms, anyone searching for us is bound to make a lot of noise. You ready?"

"What if these things have trackers or something?" Janine stuck out her foot. "They'll still come to us."

"If we're inside, GPS or whatever might have a harder time locking on precisely," Frankie said. "If we're out in the open, we're done. Let's go."

Sprinting across the parking lot, I looked to our left. Beyond the rusted remains of the chain-link fence that marked the edge of the property, granite blocks poked from a sea of dead grass. Of course the Clown Motel was next to a graveyard.

I raised my foot and kicked in the first-floor door marked OFFICE. It crashed inward, spewing white dust.

The office was dark, deserted, and filled to the brim with the highest-grade nightmare fuel. The wall behind the long reception desk featured five shelves stuffed with an army of clown dolls. Dozens of glass eyes glinted in the dusty light filtering through the broken doorway. Laughing clowns. Crying clowns. Soft plush clowns that bled through rips in their clothing. Hard porcelain clowns missing arms and legs. Clowns holding tiny drums and hamburgers and creepy-looking puppies.

I took a deep breath and immediately regretted it. The air stank like something had died inside the walls. I prayed it was just a rat or two.

"No way I'm making a last stand here," I announced to that terrifying brigade.

"With any luck, we won't have to," Frankie said, swiping a spangled clown off a wooden chair. Closing the door as best she could on the broken jamb, she angled the back of the chair beneath the knob. Meanwhile I ducked behind the reception desk—trying to keep my body as far away from the shelves as possible—and through a doorway that opened onto a second, smaller office. No creepy dolls in here: only a battered metal desk, a rolling office chair, and a set of tall lockers. That was a relief.

A second door beyond the desk led to the outside, based on the unlit EXIT sign above it. In violation of every fire regulation, a heavy steel rod pinned the latch in place. That might prevent anyone from trying to flank us.

Leaning my iron bar against the desk, I opened the

lockers until I found something excellent: a double-barreled twelve-gauge shotgun. I broke it open. Empty. In the glow from the dirt-caked windows, I read the words etched darkly on the underside of the stock: Satan's Left Hand. The weapon seemed maintained and oiled, and wonderfully old school.

The desk drawers yielded a half-full box of shotgun shells. Weapon loaded, pockets heavy with ammunition, I returned to the main office, where I found Frankie sorting through the small closet beside the reception desk. Janine stood in the middle of the room, arms crossed over her chest, tapping her elbows.

"I think we're clear back there," I said, placing what I hoped was a comforting hand on Janine's spine. "Find anything good?"

"Nobody left any cigarettes behind," Frankie said, rummaging through a dirt-smeared plastic bag filled with doll parts. "And I would literally double-tap a motherfucker for a Marlboro."

"Sounds like a great ad," I said. "'Pop a motherfucker for a Marlboro.'"

"I think this one's the worst." Frankie held up a dusty clown head, and she might have been right. The eyes had fallen out, making it look like a painted skull.

"Super. Maybe we can scare the crap out of them."

"Men outside," Janine said in a tight voice, pausing in her relentless tapping to point at the window.

Peeking between the grimy window-blinds, I saw three men standing in the bright sun beside the gas station. One hunter was Jim Marshall, of the manslaughterin' Marshall clan. Beside him stood a plump fellow with a gray moustache—I didn't recognize the face, but he was no doubt worth a lot of money. And leaning against one of the rusty gas pumps, my good neighbor Rob, looking scared in his brand-new hunting gear.

"We got contact," I said. "Three guys."

Marshall gestured at the hotel, and the three argued for a minute. Nobody pointed at my window or tried to take cover, so I assumed they had no idea they were being watched. Rob's head slumped, until Marshall reached over and snapped his fingers under Rob's nose. Rob made a halfhearted attempt to slap those fingers away and missed. Marshall laughed.

"What's going on?" Frankie asked.

"One of these guys is my neighbor."

"Someone rich actually lives on your shithole road?" Frankie said. "What'd they do, lose a bet?"

Janine stood beside me. "I knew we shouldn't have gone over for wine," she said, trying to smile.

"Hey," I said. "It was your idea. I kept trying to turn it down, remember?"

"Dumbasses," Frankie said. "Can we focus, please?"

Marshall pointed at the hotel, and the three hunters shouldered their rifles and walked in our direction. They swept their heads from side to side, fingers loose on their triggers. As if they were hunting deer, and not people. They must have known about their dead friend in the woods. Didn't they realize we had a weapon?

Retreating behind the desk, Frankie pointed her shotgun at the door. "Get the chair away," she said. "Then stand back."

"We're not killing all of them," I said, pulling the chair away from the doorknob.

Frankie squinted in the dimness. "What?"

"My neighbor. We can use him for information. He's scared, he'll talk. The other two I don't care about."

"Fine." Taking care to keep her shotgun leveled at the door, Frankie stepped from behind the desk and stood beside us at the window. "Which one is he?"

"The one who looks like he's about to shit himself." Rob, ahead of the pack, stepped onto the concrete walkway that ringed the hotel's first floor. He seemed locked on that sign announcing OFFICE. The other hunters paused in the parking lot behind him.

"How you want to play it?" Frankie asked, lowering her voice.

"I'll take point," I whispered, reversing my shotgun in my hands.

Touching my cheek as she passed, Janine disappeared behind the desk. I blew her a kiss as I moved to the door, Frankie slotting behind me, her warm hand on my shoulder. Stacked like soldiers about to raid a house, only we were headed outside, not in. In the distorted world through the peephole, Rob's hand melted and spread as he reached for the doorknob. Didn't he notice the dented wood from when I kicked the door in? These people were idiots.

The doorknob twisted.

As the door swung open, I stepped back and jabbed the shotgun hard into Rob's nose. The stock crunched bone with a sound like a barbell hitting an egg. Rob loosed a bubbly screech and fell backward.

I stepped aside so Frankie could level her weapon and pump two shots at the other hunters. Marshall's shirt vaporized in a pink mist. He stood there gurgling, confusion twisting his bland face.

Frankie pumped and fired again, and most of Marshall's

head splattered the wrecked car behind him. A chunk of door exploded beside my face, driving me back, and for a confusing half-second I thought that a dying Marshall had squeezed off a shot on reflex as he smacked the pavement. Then I saw the other hunter's head and shoulders poking above the car, along with a smoking rifle.

Frankie fired in the hunter's direction, shattering the vehicle's milky windshield but not much else, and ducked back into the office. Another rifle shot split wood near her shoulder. This guy had us pinned.

Socking my shotgun against my shoulder, I prepared to pivot into the doorway and try my luck. Move fast and smooth, fire in one motion, anticipate the target. Over the faint ringing in my ears, I heard a metallic thump, followed by scraping on concrete. The hunter's rifle boomed again, away from us.

Raising a hand for me to stop, Frankie peeked through the doorway, raised her shotgun, and fired. I stuck my head through the door in time to see the hunter flop onto the hood, wheezing like a stabbed balloon, before tumbling to the ground.

I stepped onto the walkway, shotgun leveled at the hunter's arm visible beyond the car. By the time I reached the car's fender, I could see enough of the rest of him to know that Frankie's lead had sent him to that Tax-Sheltered Penthouse in the Sky. I turned and examined the hotel from this new angle. That rear door to the office stood open, and on the ground in front of it lay a full-sized clown doll in a dusty pink jumpsuit, its head exploded in a mess of red hair and plastic bits.

Janine peeked around the rear door. "Found that big clown under the reception desk," she said. "Tossed it out.

Figured the guy would react without thinking, and he did." Stepping into the sunlight, she bent at the waist and breathed deep, touching her knees five, ten, fifteen times in loose rhythm.

"Nice one, dear," I said.

"Thanks, Janine," Frankie said, deadpan. "If only my brother had told me there was a second door, instead of just saying everything was clear, we could have flanked these fuckers in the beginning."

"I wanted to raise the difficulty level," I said. "We're having too easy a time."

"Hush," Frankie said, already looting the dead of ammunition, two radios, some energy bars, and a canteen of water. No phones, though, and no cash or identification cards. I was happy to let her sort through those wet pockets. I always preferred searching dead bodies while wearing a pair of surgical gloves, and not because I feared blood on me, or a disease. I hated the feel of cooling skin, the way muscles became watery before rigor mortis set in.

While Frankie stuffed her pockets with ammunition and energy bars, I took another look at the hunter beside the car. His wrist had an expensive watch on it, and I swallowed back my faint nausea long enough to unclasp it. I needed an upgrade for my cheap digital one. Screw you, Varney.

"Someone grab the guns?" Frankie slung the canteen onto her shoulder and picked up the radios. "Bro, drag your friend. If we're going to talk to him, we need to do it somewhere else, because the rest of these jackasses probably aren't too far behind."

VI

Dragging Rob at two hundred-plus pounds into a nearby room burned too much of my energy, and I sucked one of the canteens empty as Frankie secured the space. The windows had good sight lines of the town and the ridge beyond. If anyone was watching us from above, I hoped the two bodies in the motel parking lot would make them hesitate before heading down here.

Our three new rifles offered little comfort. Spend enough of your life fighting, and you learn that being outnumbered rarely leads to a happy outcome, unless you have air support. Setting our weapons on the bed, Frankie and I conducted an ammo check, counting up seventy rifle rounds and twenty shotgun shells. Janine flicked through channels on the radio, all of them silent. Another bad sign. Realizing their transmissions were compromised, Varney might have forced a comms blackout.

A half-dozen clown dolls crowded the shelf above the ancient television. The worst part was the bedspread, stitched with a howling Bozo face. Whoever had done the design had probably meant it as cheery, but the aging cloth left its teeth yellow. Bozo looked like he had spent the past fifty years behind the big tent smoking cigarettes and plotting to bang the drunker acrobats.

Now that we had stopped moving, my leg muscles called for a general strike, my feet tingling like tuning forks. Stuffing ammunition into my pockets, I forced my breathing into a slow rhythm, picturing my body's cells swelling with power. I needed to stay strong.

"This place is making my OCD go absolutely nuts," Janine said, plucking one of the hunting rifles off the bed and taking a position to the left of the window. She fumbled with the bolt, checked the breech, and took the safety off. I was glad for all the hours we had spent in the fields behind the house, practicing the fundamentals of shooting. Janine was an okay shot against a paper target or tin can, and I hoped she could hold her own against a human being. Her life might depend on it.

"Bro, you want to get this guy talking?" Frankie asked. "We're losing time."

I nodded, walked into the bathroom, and tried the taps of the flesh-pink sink. Nothing poured out. The room smelled of something dead, just like the office, and I refused to peek behind the shower curtain stained dark with ancient mildew. I returned to the bedroom, knelt beside Rob on the floor, and slapped him until his eyelids fluttered open.

"Howdy, neighbor," I said.

Rob started to rise, so I placed a hand against his chest and pushed until he settled back. He was a soft guy. "I'm sorry," he said, blinking rapidly, as if awakening from a dream.

"Shut up," I said.

Frankie walked over to the shelf, selected a clown doll at random, and pulled off its head like a wine cork. Holding the severed noggin so Rob could see, she asked: "How wide across you think this is? Two inches?"

Rob winced and shook his head.

"I bet I can shove it pretty far up your ass." Frankie tossed the head at Rob's chest, making him flinch. "What do you think?"

Rob whined deep in his throat.

"Good. We have some questions for you, and I expect you'll answer them." Frankie offered him a sunny smile.

Rob nodded toward me. "But he just told me to shut up."

"You know, after we get that first head up there, we'll ask you the same questions again," Frankie continued. "And if you don't feel like answering, well, that means a second creepy doll head up your colon. How many you think we can shove up there? Ten? Twelve?"

Rob shook his head harder, spraying sweat on his shirt.

Frankie bared her teeth. "Shove enough of them up there, and it'll kill you. Hard plastic, it'll break something, sepsis sets in, nasty scene. But look on the bright side: I bet you'll win some sort of prize in the morgue for weirdest body of the week."

Rob moaned. "I tell you, you won't kill me?"

Frankie shook her head.

"How do I believe you?" he asked.

"You don't have a choice," I said. "Because if you're lying, and we live through this anyway, we're going to your house and burning it down, okay? And whether or not your family is inside won't be our problem." I had no intention of carrying out any revenge on his wife, but I needed him afraid. It was just like interrogating insurgents.

"Okay." Rob nodded. "Fine. What do you want to know?"

"Do you have any cigarettes?" Frankie asked.

Janine shot my sister a dark look.

"Ignore her," I said. "Tell us how you got involved in all this crap."

"I swear, I didn't know what I was getting into at first. They felt me out. Asked my opinion on extreme sports. Talked about 'pushing my limits.' I said I liked to hunt, that I'd been on safari in Africa and stuff like that. They said they had a great stalking experience, but it'd be the sort of thing I'd never be able to talk to anyone about, if I felt comfortable with that."

"And you were comfortable," I said. "With murder."

"I swear, until just now, I didn't know we'd be hunting people. You know what they call it? Boise Longpig Hunting Club."

"What's a longpig?" Janine called out.

"It's a cannibal term for human," Frankie said. "Comes from Africa. So when did you find out you'd be committing murder for fun?"

"I told you, not until now." Rob's words tumbling out faster and faster. "They made me sign all these papers. Had me do this weird little test, you know, like a school one where you fill in the bubbles. Like a psychology thing. I kept asking what it was about, and they just said everything would be explained when the game started. I wouldn't have done it in the first place, believe me. But then my friend John? He said it was the greatest thing he'd ever done, that I had to just go with it. He said it was a spiritual experience."

"John's dead," Janine said. "He's that guy we beat to death in the woods."

"I know," Rob said. "Heard it on the radio. And you know, I don't blame you, I really don't. You had to do what you had to do, you know?"

"Spare me," I said. "How much is this little safari costing you?"

He swallowed. "A hundred grand, all of it up front."

"And what do you get at the end?" Frankie said. "One of our heads on your wall? Mounted like a fucking deer?"

Rob looked miserable. I bet he expected us to kill him. "I don't know. Like I said, I had no idea what I was getting into."

Some people are masterful liars, especially when you threaten to shove part of a creepy doll up their rear exit. Leaning down, I pulled up my pant leg so Rob could look at the bomb strapped to my ankle. "What'd they tell you about that?"

"What is that?" Rob asked.

Frankie hit him on the cheek. It was a soft blow, open-handed, but Rob yelped as if she had knocked out his teeth. I almost laughed, it was so dramatic.

"You baby," Janine snorted.

"You know what it is," I said. "No way they sent you in here without telling you about the bombs strapped to us. They tell you not to get too close?"

Rob shook his head. "I swear, they didn't tell us anything."

That seemed odd. If these people were paying a hundred thousand dollars apiece for the privilege of playing the most dangerous game, why hadn't the organizers warned them that their prey might explode into little bits of shrapnel and bone?

Frankie mimed snapping on a surgical glove.

"Not yet," I told her.

Frankie lowered her arm. "You're no fun."

"They tell you anything else about the game?" I asked

Rob. "Rules, anything like that?"

"Just that it's the whole day, and there were three of you, and we hunt until you're down. They said if we didn't find all of you, that was okay, because there were searchers, tough guys, who would finish up." Rob's lips quavered. "I'm sorry, okay? I had no idea. These security guys they're using, I think they're neo-Nazis or something."

"Sorry doesn't do squat for us," Janine said. "Didn't you think we'd fight back? That we'd get a gun or something?"

"They said we weren't in any real danger," Rob said, pointing at me. "They said he was a drunk, that he was in the military once but lost his skills. It'd be good sport but we weren't at risk."

"Good sport." My cheeks burned. "I went to your house. You know I'm not an alcoholic."

"You drank a lot," Rob said, his voice shrill. "And then you ran out. What was I supposed to think?"

"What about us?" Janine said.

"They said there were two girls, too." Rob lowered his eyes to the smudged carpet. "They said you wouldn't be trouble at all."

Frankie stepped forward and drove a fist into Rob's jaw, twisting her hips for added momentum. As Rob screeched and clutched his mouth, she bent close and hissed: "This 'girl' has killed a lot of men. And they were a lot tougher than you. Understand me, boy?" With that, she placed a palm on his forehead and pushed, banging the back of his head against the floor.

"Your house sucked, by the way," Janine said. "You have no fucking taste, you slippery elitist fuck."

I had an idea. Maybe a stupid one. Borrowing a radio

from Janine, I asked Rob: "Which channel?"

He named it. I set the channel, and the speaker burped static when I pressed the button. "Varney," I said. "Hey, boy."

Frankie rolled her eyes, and I winked at her.

"What you want?" Varney replied. The signal was weak, his words accented with static.

"Got one of your guys," I said, prodding Rob with my toe. "So I think we're going to do a little negotiating. How's that sound?"

A long pause. "Proof of life," Varney said.

I pressed the button and angled the speaker toward Rob. "Say something good."

"Something good," Rob said.

"That work for you?" I asked Varney.

Another burst of static, long enough for me to start wondering if I had somehow overplayed my hand. I glanced at my ankle and its heavy strap, the little button glowing on that black box. If Varney set it off, would I have time to feel the explosion before my life winked out?

"Okay," Varney asked. "One life for one life. Give him up, one of you walks free. You have my word."

"Sorry, dude," I said. "I don't exactly take you at your word. How about you deactivate these things on our ankles, make it a fair fight?"

"How do we know you'll keep your word?"

"How do I know you'll keep yours? Deactivate these things, and your boy here walks."

"Where are you now?"

"You're so funny. Deactivate. You don't have a choice. You detonate, and your boy dies anyway. He's right next to me. You have thirty seconds."

I stood and waited, counting in my head. When I reached nineteen, the red light on my ankle flickered and died. Frankie retreated to the bathroom, where she climbed into the tub. Janine looked at her quizzically, but I nodded my appreciation. If something went wrong and the bomb detonated, the porcelain would absorb most of the blast. Taking a deep breath and holding it, Frankie jabbed her fingers into her own loop with the ferocity of a coyote chewing its leg free of a trap, peeling back wires and canvas.

"You get it off?" I called.

"Yeah, no problem," she called through the open doorway. "I still think you gave away our leverage."

"How do you mean?" I said. Although every fiber of my being screamed at me to tear away my own bomb, I wanted to keep an eye on Rob. Although he stayed quiet on the floor, his breathing had slowed, a little color seeping back into his cheeks. I could sense him calculating the odds.

"Despite my precautions back there, I'm not totally convinced these things are wired to blow. I think they're a trick to keep us locked in a tight area," she said, returning to the bedroom. "Otherwise they would have told numb-nuts here that we're potentially explosive, keep their distance."

I heard a click behind me. "There's a little screw that pops out," Janine said. "Right behind that black box." Her loop dropped to the rug.

"It was the only thing I could negotiate," I said, defensive. "No way they'd let us out of here."

Frankie tossed her loop on the bed. Rubbing her ankle, she turned to Rob. "You don't have a phone on you."

Rob shook his head.

"What did they do with it?" I asked.

"You saw where we were, on the river?" Rob asked. "They took our phones, put them in a lockbox in one of those SUVs. Said we'd get them back after the hunt concludes."

Frankie scooped a shotgun off the bed and pointed it at Rob while I worked on freeing my ankle. Following Janine's directions, I pried loose the proper screw, and the loop unraveled in my hands. I tossed it away like a dead snake.

Varney had fulfilled his side of the bargain. Did we tie up Rob and leave him? Take him with us, just in case he came in useful later?

Frankie solved the conundrum for me by yanking a stained pillow from beneath Bozo the comforter. Rob barely had time to scream before she dropped the pillow on his face, jammed the barrel of her shotgun deep into its softness, and pulled the trigger.

The pillow exploded in a cloud of pink feathers. My eardrums whined as the shot clapped off the tight walls. Frankie stepped back, her face speckled in red. "Damn, louder than I thought it'd be," she called out, shaking her head back and forth.

"Why did you do that?" I asked.

"Why wouldn't I do that?" she said, reloading the shotgun. "I'm being humane here."

"What?"

"What was I supposed to do, suffocate him?" Frankie handed her weapon to me. "Never tried that with a pillow before. Doesn't do squat, in terms of blocking noise. Janine, anything out there?"

"I don't see anything," Janine said, locked on the desert beyond the window. I debated whether to tell her about the juicy scrap of Rob on her shoulder blade.

"Good," Frankie said, disappearing into the bathroom. She returned with a threadbare towel, which she used to clean her face and shoulders. "Maybe we got lucky for once. Bro, you okay?"

Borrowing her towel, I wiped at the feathers that had settled on my chest, leaving little red smears. "I gave them my word," I said, so softly that Frankie cupped a hand behind her ear to hear better.

"And you're a man of your word," she said, patting me on the shoulder. "I'm very proud of you. But they didn't make any kind of deal with me. So grab two guns, pretty please."

I did as ordered, choosing a bolt-action .308 with a shiny scope. It came with a padded strap that felt good on my shoulder. I also selected my double-barrel shotgun, noting a bit of Rob's blood on the walnut stock. I hoped I would never have to meet Rob's wife again. What was her name?

"What do we do now?" Janine asked. Gravity had begun to pull that loose speck of flesh down her shirt, leaving a bloody smear in its wake.

"Run for it." Walking over, I flicked at Janine's back, sending the meat across the room to spatter on a clown doll's nose.

"What are you doing?" Janine asked, trying to peek over her shoulder. Aside from the muscle twitching beneath her left eye, she seemed okay.

"Nothing," I said. "Just some random debris."

The radio in my hand crackled again. "You there?" Varney asked.

I hit the button. "Yeah."

"You bringing our boy back?"

"Where do you want him?"

"Where are you now?"

"I'm an idiot but not stupid," I said. "You want your boy or not?"

A pause so long I wondered if Varney had decided to call my bluff. I looked at Janine, who turned to the window and shook her head. Nobody around. They must have known about the other dead men. Were they watching the motel from a distance?

"Yes, I do," Varney said.

"Okay," I said, and told him where to go. "Your guy will be there in ninety minutes. We're going to make him walk. Meanwhile, we're heading for the exit as fast as we can."

And with that, I lowered the volume of the radio and slipped it back in my pocket. I had sounded so capable, and yet I felt so weak.

VII

Before we left the motel, Frankie ransacked every drawer in the room, finding a paper matchbook in the bedside drawer. She struck a match, lit the pack, and dropped the flickering meteor on the bedspread. Bozo blackened at the edges, smile yawning to blackness. "Place this creepy doesn't deserve to stay standing," she said.

After some internal debate, I took the three ankle loops with us. We hooked a left outside the motel, squeezing down a narrow path between the flank of the building and the graveyard. We passed a stretch of tombstones choked by desert brush, and I tossed one of the loops as far as I could over the ruined fence.

"What are you doing?" Janine asked.

"If there's GPS in these," I said, "it'll hopefully confuse the hell out of them."

The town beyond the motel had surrendered to nature: the wooden buildings splintering and caving in, a few small trees sprouting from shattered windows, the road beneath our feet cracked like desert hardpan. We circuited around a hole so deep its bottom escaped sunlight, where I paused to deposit another loop. I hurled the final one through the open window of a particularly rickety-looking house at the end of the block, hoping against hope that the whole structure might collapse on whoever entered it first.

"That place you said they could pick up your neighbor," Frankie said.

"Just wait," I replied. "We might get lucky."

I kept thinking about what Frankie said, how the loops might have been an elaborate ruse, a way to keep us trapped through the power of our own fear. She might have been right, but Varney also struck me as a straight-forward kind of dude. Maybe he would hit a button when he discovered that my agreement with him was bullshit, and parts of this ghost town would explode to dust.

We stayed low, moving fast, and soon found ourselves at the ragged edge of town. We knelt in the shadow of a low brick building, out of sight of the ridge. A black column of smoke stained the blue sky, as wood and plastic and a thousand creepy clowns burned to ash.

"We could find another building," Janine said. "Lay low, sneak out at night."

"Hold on, I can feel this crap drying," Frankie said, pulling her left sleeve over her hand and wiping at the last spots of blood on her forehead. "Anyway, that's not a bad idea. But those guys who took us last night? We try and hide, they'll probably send them in. We can't fight night vision, thermal scopes, whatever they got."

"I wonder if they've taken casualties before," I said.

"If we live through this," Frankie said, "we can Google whether any rich people have died in Idaho hunting accidents over the past couple years. If anything pops up, I bet those are it. Sure, you can disappear a random person, but getting rid of someone famous takes a lot of work."

"I can think of a couple of celebrities I want disap-peared," Janine said.

I pictured an annoying pop star, dressed in the flimsiest of stage costumes, shrieking as she ran through the woods, pursued by a small army of men with rifles. Before today, I might have found that funny.

"Let's give it a few minutes," I said. "Then we head for the woods over there. Climb the ridge but take it wide."

"Does that jibe with your absurd plan?" Frankie asked.

"It better," I said. "We don't have a choice."

I had a better sense of the land now. The ridge steepened to our left, offering superior elevation over the part we had crossed earlier. The slope in that area was more thickly forested than where we had descended, and I hoped there was a path to the top that we could navigate with our heavy rifles. Added bonus: we would likely avoid anyone entering town along our original path, or the road.

"It's weird that this all comes back to Dad," I said.

"I don't know, didn't really surprise me," Frankie said. "Final crappy gift from a crappy father."

"You shut your mouth," I shot back.

"Guys," Janine muttered.

"I know you got some hero worship for him," Frankie rumbled. "And that's fine, you're a boy, I get that. When Mom left, he had zero idea how to raise a teenage girl. None. Probably one of the reasons I turned out like I did."

"You're responsible for your own mistakes," I said.

"Oh, okay." Frankie sniffed, blinking rapidly. "You know how bad he ignored me? I tried getting his attention by making him a wooden beer-can holder in shop class. Remember that? Like if I helped with his drinking, he might actually talk to me."

"Guys," Janine said, her voice urgent. Her hands in her lap squeezed into fists, the knuckles straining white against the skin.

"What?" I turned to her.

"We're running out of time." My wife, right as usual.

It took us an hour to scale the ridge. We did it slow, sticking beneath the trees, taking our time so our feet would kick up as few rocks as possible. Every few minutes we stopped and scanned the trees around us for sound or movement. Frankie climbed the slope like a goat, switching her shotgun from hand to hand whenever she needed a better grip on a rock or root, while Janine moved without pause, breathing hard, humming a low tune under her breath. Meanwhile I poured so much sweat it made my insoles squish every time I took a step. I was fine with Frankie staying far ahead of me.

I felt bad about Rob. His face kept flickering into view, frightened, paler than the pillow dropped on it. We could have knocked him out, tied him up, and left him outside for Varney and the others to find. The sight of violence had neutralized him as a threat long before Frankie pulled the trigger.

In Iraq, I quickly learned how to force those kinds of thoughts into a dungeon in my mind. Now I shoved Rob down there with a lot of dead Iraqis and Zombie Bill's men. My wife and sister needed me, and so did my child. If people had to die to ensure their safety, so be it.

Near the top, we stopped for a panoramic view of the town. Flames poured from the windows of the clown motel, blackening the white walls. My nostrils flared with the stench of burning plastic, scorched hair. The high sun reflected off the windshield of a black SUV creeping down the road at walking pace. It stopped beside the graveyard, and a dark speck emerged from the driver's side. Too far to tell from this distance if it was Varney.

Frankie tapped me on the shoulder. "Sorry," she said.

"I'm the one who's sorry." I placed my hand over hers. "You're the best sister."

"It's not Dad's fault. He was doing the right thing at the time."

"I know. Let's keep climbing."

At the top of the ridge, the river came into view, a shimmering silver line that curved into the rocky valley where we had started the hunt. From this vantage, we had no sightline on the gravel shore where the hunters had assembled, but something told me the cars were there, parked and waiting. Hopefully without too many people standing guard.

I looked to our right. Impossible to see much through the trees. I pulled the radio out of my pocket and hit the button. "You there, Varney?"

A crackle. "Yes."

"We just put him in that shed, underneath the first tarp. We left him tied up. We beat him pretty good but so what, he'll live." I wished I could see the shed from here. They would surround it in a few minutes.

"Stand by," Varney said. I had no intention of doing any such thing. Gesturing to my wife and sister, we began to pick our way down the opposite side of the ridge, toward the river and salvation.

We had made it maybe a hundred yards when I heard—or imagined I heard—a faint scream coming from the direction of the shed. While I don't like to think of myself as a sadist, the idea of a hunter reaching under one of those tarps and finding a new fanged friend cheered me right up. With a bit more bounce in my step, I veered us onto a faint cut that ran through the trees, angling toward the river.

With any luck, we had sown enough panic and confusion to give us a fighting chance at finding a phone and a car. I could almost imagine us getting out of this alive. And maybe that thought made me lift my head a little too high, or walk through the brush a little too loudly—

Beside my head, a rock cracked.

My cheek burned, prickling.

On instinct I dropped to the dirt, my shotgun clattering beside me. In my peripheral vision I saw Fred the Nazi Marlboro Man standing on an outcrop to our right, his old-fashioned revolver held in a two-handed Weaver stance, drawing a bead on us.

I reached for my shotgun, and my hand scraped earth.

A flicker in the corner of my eye. I knew what it meant. I slapped my hands over my ears as the shotgun boomed, Janine pointing and firing like a pro.

The buckshot caught Fred in the side, his shirt blossoming red as he stumbled back. Janine pulled the trigger again, and his chest seemed to implode. He tumbled onto the rocks, his revolver clattering away.

Removing my hands from my ears, I stood and hugged Janine as tightly as I could, making sure to avoid the hot barrel of the shotgun as I did so. Her body trembled against mine. I cupped a hand over the back of her neck, her pulse fluttering quick against the tips of my fingers.

"It's okay," I said. "You did the only thing."

I hoped the words would help.

Janine dropped the shotgun and sank her face into my shirt and made a low sound like an animal dying. I pulled her in and held on. After my first kill, that Baghdad boy too young to be carrying a rifle, I had vomited until my stomach turned inside-out. "Whatever happens, don't barf on me," I said.

She laughed, or it might have been a sob.

Frankie worked on the corpse, turning out any pockets still intact after that double-load of buckshot. "Move fast," she said. "Chances are good they heard that one."

The body yielded a wallet, a radio, a full speed-loader along with a few loose rounds, what looked like a key fob, and, praise Glory, a phone. Frankie yelled with glee and flicked it on.

"Signal?" I asked.

"Waking up," she said, before grimacing. "No signal."

"I'm okay." Janine stepped back, one hand still on my chest, wiping her eyes with the other.

Just wait, I almost told her. You think you're okay, with that adrenaline barreling through your veins like meth. Only later come the nightmares. Are you ready for that, baby?

The dead man's radio crackled. This time I recognized Baker's voice. "Fred?" he asked. "We're hearing shots, Fred. Position?"

I pressed the button. "You keep giving me hostages, man."

"You let him go right now, or you're dead," Baker said. "And we'll make you suffer to your last breath. No negotiation, no compromise."

"Yawn," I replied. "One of your other guests gave us this hunting rifle with a cool scope? You want to wave for me?" I had no angle on our hunters in the forest below, of course, but the mental image of Baker cringing was its own reward.

Frankie gestured for us to keep moving, and I raised a

finger for her to wait. I retrieved Fred's six-shooter, emptied the spent loads, and reloaded the cylinder. The weapon felt nice and comforting in my hands. I bet it was in top condition. Maybe I would keep it as a trophy if we escaped this place with our lives.

Janine picked up the shotgun, and we returned to the trees. I found myself thinking about my daddy during his big gunfight, if he had panicked as he shot those men, or if he had stayed a cool customer throughout. I hoped for the latter, drawing a little strength from the image of him as a cowboy avenger, calm and resolute under fire. Our family, we don't fold under pressure, and we die with our teeth in the last enemy's throat.

It seemed peaceful enough for me to take Janine's hand. "I'm sorry," I said.

She squeezed back. "For what?"

"All this. It is my family's fault, in a weird way. You were right." I was keenly aware of Frankie, ten yards ahead of us, turning to shoot me a look of death.

"I still love you," Janine said. "I'm sorry for getting harsh at the hotel."

"Dumbasses," Frankie hissed, pointing left. "We need to change paths."

We picked up a narrow trail that wound along the edge of a steep cliff over the river. Thickets of young trees screened us from the far side, but every few minutes I caught sight of the gravel shore and an SUV parked at its edge. A solitary figure stood near the front bumper. After a quarter mile or so, I could view the land beyond the beach: a dirt road meandered away from the water toward a cut in the cliffs. Two more shadows in the swaying grass beside the road. Maybe nothing, maybe more men. No sign of the second SUV, or that black jeep carrying men in suits.

The radio crackled again. "Let's make a deal," Baker said.

Varney broke onto the channel. "What the hell?"

Probably a trap, I thought. Fake an argument, set us up. "I'm listening," I told the radio.

"We got a man with a snake bite here," Baker said. "And you eliminated a few of our other men, besides. How about we call a truce, let you walk out of here?"

"So you're saying we won?" I asked.

"Fuck you," Varney broke in.

"I'm saying it's a truce," Baker said. "Now we're going to leave. You're free to do what you want. You breathe a word of this to anyone, and we'll kill you, understand?"

Beside me, Frankie shook her head. "What about that family grudge?" I asked. "All those years of bad blood? You're just going to let that go?"

"For now."

I turned off the radio and pocketed it without bothering to reply. As we walked, Janine rubbed my spine. It felt good. The path descended, and in a few minutes, we found ourselves a little downstream from the SUV. A rotted log, thick with moss and mushrooms, offered a convenient spot to crouch behind.

I had a better view of the man leaning against the hood. The harsh sunlight made it hard to tell a face. The range was maybe fifty yards and I could hit him with the rifle pretty easily. The river was shallow here, a few inches of water skimming over a bed of gray shale, and after I shot him, we could cross to the other side.

I lifted the rifle to my eye and sighted. The man stood perfectly still, unmoving. His features came into perfect focus through the scope: the square jaw scruffed with the faint beginnings of a beard, the narrow forehead, the boxer's nose. I felt a faint thump on the log as Frankie placed her barrel beside mine, ready to back my play. After I shot the first guard, the others in the grass would come running.

I focused on my breathing, timing the shot for the bottom of my exhale. My finger skimmed the trigger when I felt Janine tap my back.

I followed my wife's finger upstream, toward the woods at the base of the ridge. A scrum of men tore from the forest, in a blur of orange vests and camouflage and rifles, carrying what looked like one of those dusty tarps from the shed. Varney led them, in his black jacket, yelling into what looked like a satellite phone. As they picked their way down a path beside the river, the right honorable Ted Ryan appeared at the rear of the group, holding three black bands in his left hand. I guess our leg-loops had GPS chips after all.

The rear door of the SUV opened, and Baker stepped onto the riverbank, waving frantically at the approaching group.

"Too bad we don't have the Monkey Man," I whispered to Frankie. "He'd fix all this up right quick."

Frankie chuckled. "That he would. That he would. But maybe he's here in spirit."

I looked over. "What do you mean?"

Frankie held up Fred's key fob. "Notice anything weird?"

That little bit of plastic lacked a car company's logo, but otherwise it seemed ordinary. I shook my head.

"You spent a lot of time in Baghdad, bro."

Then I understood. "Guess we'll see who's right about

bluffing," I said.

"What's going on?" Janine asked.

"Plug your ears, babe," I said, activating my radio. "Baker."

Baker lifted his radio. "Yes?"

"Don't play me for an idiot. You have no intention of letting us live, right?"

The group had reached the SUV. Five overweight, sweating men muscled the screaming dude in the sheet into the back of the car as Varney stood a few feet away, scanning the ridges and cliffs for movement. From this distance, I saw Baker snarl like a wounded coyote. "You're right," he said. "Sooner or later, we're going to kill you."

"That's what I thought," I said, and nodded to Frankie, who pressed the button on the key fob.

VIII

When all this was over, I would return home and fish that little silver necklace out of my gun safe. I would find a shovel and walk out back, past the yard and the fence, into the fields. There was a good spot where the land rose slightly, with a panoramic view of the river and the taller hills of Oregon beyond. I would dig a hole and bury the necklace and say a few words to remember a girl I had never known until she showed up dead in my house. I would say something for the boy who had tried so hard to live before these bastards ended him on the floor of a gas station. The ritual would do them no good, but it might convince me for a few days that a certain order existed in the world, and that sometimes it would produce something like justice, if you worked hard enough.

After a few days, I knew, that feeling would fade. My kid would come home, Janine and I would tie the knot for the second time, and life would roll on. Do you know what happens to the blood on your hands? It washes off, and don't let anyone tell you different.

IX

The explosion was enormous, crumpling the side of the SUV like a soda can hit by a sledgehammer. The shockwave blurred a white arc across the river and slammed my eardrums into the middle of my skull, and when I stood, a wave of dizziness threatened to topple me over. Frankie said something, but the words sounded distorted, almost electronic.

It was raining metal and bits of people.

I bent over and breathed until my stomach settled. The ringing faded enough to hear the roar of the river unperturbed. With Janine and Frankie in my wake, I splashed toward the burning SUV, passing at the shoreline a smoking pair of boots with the feet still in them.

The heat from the fires baked my face and arms. I scanned the beach for any survivors. Our leg loops had turned the SUV into an enormous bomb, generating a hurricane of shrapnel that had shredded everyone. I spied Varney, mangled to hamburger. Janine kicked his smoking leg as she passed, and smiled at me. It made me feel proud and a little scared.

Frankie circled the burning vehicle, crouched low in case any survivors took a shot, and plunged into the grass beyond the beach. I gestured for Janine to stay on our side of the SUV. Over the roar of flames and the sizzle of engine fluids, I heard Frankie talking in calm tones. She reappeared with a satellite phone pressed to her ear. She was reciting names, coordinates, issues. The cavalry was on its way, probably wearing a creepy mask.

"Can we clean this?" I asked, once Frankie lowered the phone.

She sighed. "Sure can. My people are coming, but we should probably hide out until they arrive, just in case. I owe you an apology, by the way. I guess they weren't bluffing about the bombs."

"You can buy me a beer."

We heard a low groan from the edge of the riverbank. I saw a pile of blackened clothes, half-submerged, thrashing against the current. Baker, or what was left of him.

I trotted over for a better look. He had managed to twist his body so part of his face poked above the surface of the water, his chin and cheekbone studded with bits of shiny black metal. Most of his hair had burned away. As I knelt beside him, his one good eye found me. He was fading fast.

"Didn't see this coming, huh?" I said.

Baker gurgled and blew pinkish bubbles.

"So what do we win?" I asked, as his curtain descended. "Anything cool?"

ACKNOWLEDGMENTS

I've spent a lot of time in Idaho over the past several years. It's beautiful country, well worth visiting, and I've had no better guides than Robert Baldwin, Matt Baldwin, Brittani Lee, and the rest of my family out there. To good friends like Arlie, Jared, and everyone else around Boise—I owe you a sizable debt, as well.

I also want to thank Eric Campbell, Lance Wright, and the whole pirate crew at Down & Out Books. Chris Rhatigan's eagle eyes made the drafts stronger. Beers are on me, next time around.

This book was largely written to the peerless tunes of The Handsome Family and Nick Cave. I hope at least some of their verbal virtuosity rubbed off on my prose.

Nick Kolakowski is the author of the Love & Bullets Hookup series of crime novellas. His short fiction has appeared in *Thuglit*, *Shotgun Honey*, *Plots with Guns*, and various anthologies. He lives and writes in New York City.

NickKolakowski.com

DOWN & OUT BOOKS

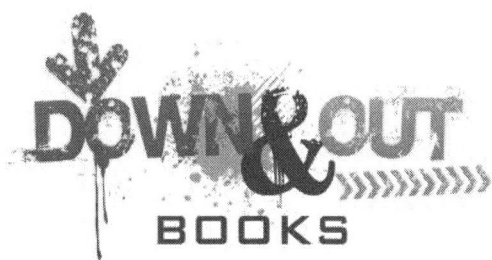

On the following pages are a few
more great titles from the
Down & Out Books publishing family.

For a complete list of books and to
sign up for our newsletter,
go to DownAndOutBooks.com.

ABC
GROUP DOCUMENTATION

ALL DUE RESPECT

SHOTGUN HONEY

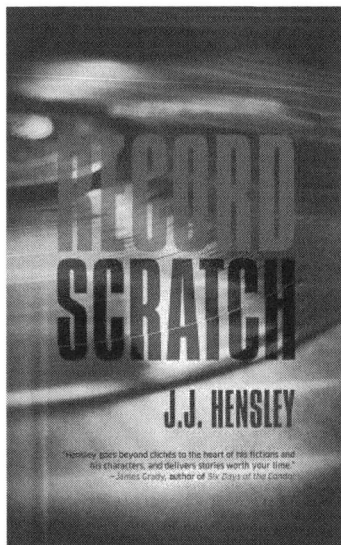

Record Scratch
A Trevor Galloway Thriller
J.J. Hensley

Down & Out Books
October 2018
978-1-948235-35-8

Somewhere there exists a vinyl record with twelve songs recorded by the legendary Jimmy Spartan. Trevor Galloway has been
hired to solve Spartan's murder and recover his final songs.

When his client terminates their first meeting by taking her own
life, Galloway's journey takes him into the arms of an old
flame, the crosshairs of familiar enemies, and past the demons
in his own mind.

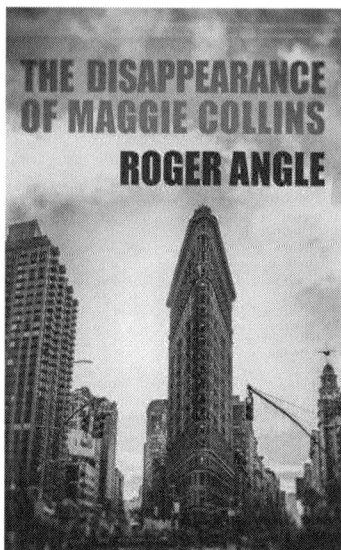

The Disappearance of Maggie Collins
Roger Angle

Down & Out Books
October 2018
978-1-946502-19-3

Maggie is a hot young mixed-race NYPD detective, half Puerto Rican, half black and all bombshell. Love and lust follow her wherever she goes. She volunteers to go undercover to catch a serial killer.

"Don't get in the car," her lieutenant says. But of course, she gets into the car.

The killer thinks he is in love, but his idea of love is a little strange.

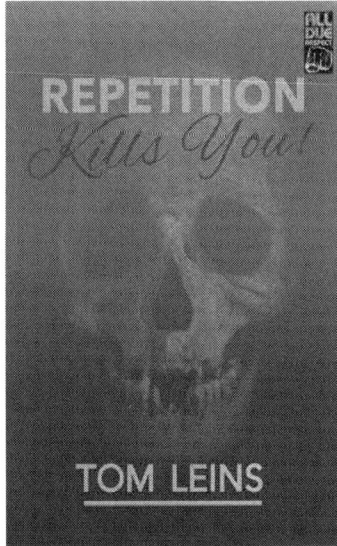

Repetition Kills You
Stories by Tom Leins

All Due Respect, an imprint of
Down & Out Books
September 2018
978-1-948235-28-0

Repetition Kills You comprises 26 short stories, presented in alphabetical order, from 'Actress on a Mattress' to 'Zero Sum'. The content is brutal and provocative: small-town pornography, gun-running, mutilation and violent, blood-streaked stories of revenge. The cast list includes sex offenders, serial killers, bare-knuckle fighters, carnies and corrupt cops. And a private eye with a dark past—and very little future.

Welcome to Paignton Noir.

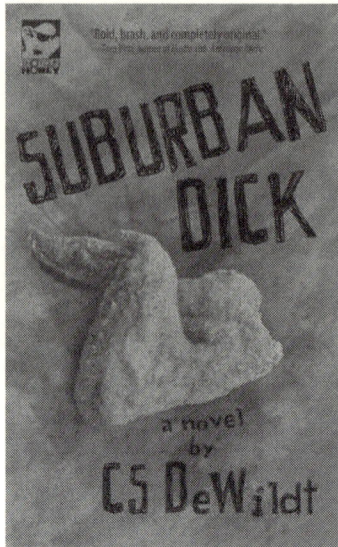

Suburban Dick
CS DeWildt

Shotgun Honey, an imprint of
Down & Out Books
978-1-946502-72-8

When private eye/deadbeat dad Gus Harris catches a new case, he hopes it will not only save his failing PI agency, but also his family. However, a straight forward missing persons case quickly spirals into a dangerous world of high school wrestlers, embezzlement, and murder.

Solving the case isn't the issue, it's keeping his family safe from the fallout.

Made in the USA
Middletown, DE
09 January 2021